Jessica Vitalis

Greenwillow Books
An Imprint of HarperCollinsPublishers

The text of this book is set in 11.5 Sabon LT Std.
Book design by Paul Zakris

Library of Congress Cataloging-in-Publication Data

Names: Vitalis, Jessica, author.
Title: Coyote queen / by Jessica Vitalis.
Description: First edition. |
New York : Greenwillow Books, an imprint of HarperCollinsPublishers, [2023] |
Audience: Ages 8-12. | Audience: Grades 4-6. |
Summary: Desperate for the prize money to escape her mother's abusive boyfriend, twelve-year-old Fud enters a beauty pageant, but her eerie connection to nearby coyotes helps her see who she is meant to be, and who she can truly save.
Identifiers: LCCN 2023014347 | ISBN 9780063314405 (hardback) |
ISBN 9780063314429 (ebook)
Subjects: CYAC: Family violence—Fiction. | Human-animal communication—Fiction. | Coyote—Fiction. | Mobile home living—Fiction. | Beauty contests—Fiction.
Classification: LCC PZ7.1.V595 Co 2023 | DDC [Fic]—dc23
LC record available at https://lccn.loc.gov/2023014347
23 24 25 26 27 LBC 5 4 3 2 1
First Edition

Greenwillow Books

To every kid searching the dark
for a glimmer of light

CHAPTER ONE

Before the coyote stuff happened, I would have told you that magic didn't exist. If it did, I would have used it to win the lottery. Or make a genie in a bottle grant me three wishes. Or find a fairy godmother—anything to improve the crummy life Mom and I were living.

That doesn't mean I sat around crying about how things were, because I didn't. And I certainly didn't think twice about magic. I was too practical for that. As far as I was concerned, nothing happened in the world that couldn't be explained by science.

Now I know better. I might look like a normal girl on the outside, but on the inside . . . well, let me put it this way: if you consider yourself the practical sort, then this is one story that you're going to find really hard to believe.

I pushed the world's oldest vacuum around the shaggy speckled carpet from the Stone Ages, taking care to make straight, even lines. The first time I vacuumed Larry's trailer, I did it all helter-skelter, and when he saw it, he made me do twenty push-ups and then re-vacuum the whole place. He said it was for my own good—that a little discipline now would turn me into a productive adult later. I expected Mom to step in, but she only shrugged and said a little discipline couldn't hurt.

I stopped to push the curls from my face and wipe a stream of sweat dripping from my forehead.

We had every window in the trailer open and a fan blowing, but all that did was suck in more of the hot Wyoming air from outside. The apartment Mom and I lived in before she met Larry had an actual air conditioner—one that sat in the window blowing a steady stream of cool air. It didn't turn the place into a freezer, but it was a whole lot better than baking in this oven.

Not that I was complaining. Or I shouldn't have been, anyway.

That last apartment was in the basement of a building on a really busy street. I woke up once to see some guy with his face pressed against the glass, watching me sleep through a crack in the shades. Mom said he was probably harmless, but I had trouble sleeping after that. Out here, there's nothing but tumbleweeds as far as the eye can see.

Well, okay, there's the empty trailer in the lot next to us, and the old, rusted-out tractor sitting across the dirt road at the end of our driveway, and a whole heap of junk spread out around the property, but that's it—no other houses, gas stations, grocery stores, or schools. Nobody poking their noses in our business, which Larry said was a good thing.

I wasn't sure what business we had, but at least no one was around to make fun of the faded T-shirts Mom bought me at yard sales, with logos from Kidz Kamp and Camp Teton and all the other places rich kids spend their summers.

"Fud, what're you doing?" Mom yelled from the kitchen, which officially started where the carpet ended and the dingy linoleum began. "Get back to work."

She wanted everything perfect when Larry got home, even if we couldn't do anything about the hole he'd punched in the wall or the water damage on the ceiling.

She probably would've walked over to tell me except her arms were elbow deep in dirty dishwater. Usually the dishes were my job, but she'd baked all afternoon, and I doubted there was a single clean dish left in the whole place, so she said she'd take care of it while I finished the vacuuming.

I strained to get the vacuum moving again. On the television at the Laundromat, there were always commercials where the woman (It was always a woman, which I thought was stupid. Didn't men know how to vacuum?) pushed around a light-as-air vacuum with one hand. Sometimes, the vacuums didn't even have cords! This vacuum was nothing like that. It was more like a spaceship—a hunk of metal so huge it could probably launch a person to the moon.

As I moved forward and back around the lumpy couch and the worn recliner no one but Larry was allowed to sit in, I smelled the chocolate cake baking in the oven. Larry would be home from work soon. He claimed he didn't eat sweets on account of his training to get back in the ring (apparently the empty HoHos packages I saw in the trash every morning didn't count), but it was his birthday, so Mom had splurged on groceries and made him an all-natural cake out of carob and honey.

I didn't know why you'd eat chocolate cake of any kind if you cared about being healthy, but whatever. I couldn't wait to see the look on his face when she brought it out. And I *really* couldn't wait to have a piece. Even though this wasn't one of the fancy, store-bought cakes that I'd always longed to try, you couldn't really go wrong when it came to chocolate cake.

With a little luck, Larry would be in a good mood.

"You're the ref in my ring," he'd say to Mom, breaking into a real grin, and not the kind he gave when he thought someone was an idiot and he was about to make sure they knew it. Then he'd say a bunch of other goofy things like "You're the tape on my knuckles" and "You're the gloves on my fists" and Mom would giggle and raise her hand up to cover the snaggled front tooth she'd never had the money to fix.

And then they'd kiss, which would be gross, but he'd be happy and tell us stories from when he was the middleweight boxing champion of Wyoming and Nebraska. I loved his stories even though I was never quite sure if they were true. (I searched online once. I couldn't find a single article about him biting someone's ear off in the ring, although there was an article about another boxer who did that.) He'd sit for hours, drinking his Bud Light and spinning yarns about all the men he'd whupped.

Sometimes, Mom let me stay up late and listen. Other times—usually when he got to a story about how he kicked someone's can outside the ring—she told me it was time to shower even if I'd showered the night before. She was just trying to get rid of me because she didn't think fighting was the answer to all the world's problems, but she didn't dare say that in front of Larry or she'd end up in a fight herself.

After we finished cleaning the trailer, Mom took a shower and changed into a pretty summer dress with butterflies. The dress used to be dark purple, but it had been washed so many times that it was now more of a soft lilac. There were some loose threads hanging off the hem. I didn't say anything because her white face was paler than anyone should ever be at the end of summer, but she'd brushed her hair until it shone. She'd even put on lip gloss, trying to look her best.

I didn't care about looking my best, which was a good thing because instead of Mom's straight blond hair I had a mess of dark, wispy waves that had a mind of their own. And where Mom's eyes were dark brown with a golden ring that glowed like honey in the sunlight, mine were plain brown and more like something you might find at the bottom of the toilet, if you know what I mean.

The one thing I had going for me was my golden-brown skin, which made me look tan even in the middle of winter. Mom said I got that from my dad, who was from Spain and had come to the US to visit relatives when they met. I wanted to know more about him, but Mom said that was all she knew. She also said that anyone could be a donor, but being a father had to be earned, and mine had given up that chance when he'd disappeared after finding out she was pregnant.

Mom took a break from making dinner to inspect my outfit. I tugged at my T-shirt. She always bought my clothes a couple of sizes too big so I'd have plenty of room to grow, but this one had become tight around the chest over the summer. Since she hadn't been to the Laundromat lately, it was the only clean shirt I could find.

She smiled and pulled me in for a hug.

I let myself relax into her arms. She'd always towered over me, but a recent growth spurt meant I'd finally caught up. Even though we were both tall, Mom was little more than skin and bones, while I'd developed curves I wished would disappear.

I breathed in her peppermint scent. I couldn't remember the last time she'd hugged me this way—just her and me.

"Thanks for your help today," she said.

Something in my chest melted. I wanted to stay wrapped up in her arms forever, but the roar of Larry's truck and the crunch of wheels in the driveway announced his arrival. Mom broke away. The softness under my ribs turned sharp and prickly. Mom and I used to be two halves that made a perfect whole. Now it was like Larry was the whole, and the two of us weren't worth measuring.

Sometimes, I thought about running away. But life before Larry was spent moving from one lousy apartment to another, camping out in the car when we couldn't come up with enough cash for a deposit and first month's rent, not knowing how long we might have to make a single can of ravioli last. I had twenty bucks I'd found in an empty dryer at the Laundromat, but that wouldn't get me far. If Mom couldn't make it with her waitressing job, what hope did I have on my own?

So when Larry stomped up the stairs and pulled open the door, I put on my best smile and yelled, "Happy Birthday!"

He stepped back like he was surprised and looked

around, pretending to be confused. "Birthday?" he said. "Does someone around here have a birthday?"

His face and hands were heavily tanned from all the time he spent outside at work. His arms were nearly as white as his T-shirt on account of the jumpsuit he wore to keep the mine's trash off his clothes.

I could see he was in a good mood by the way he casually hooked a thumb through the loop of his jeans. My worry slipped away as I said, "You do!" at the same time that Mom told him she'd fixed his favorite dinner. He pulled off his steel-toed work boots and lined them up on the mat next to the door before he sank down at the square table in the kitchen.

"Beer?" I asked.

"Bud Light," he said, but I was already pulling a can from the fridge because of course I knew that, and it wasn't like we had anything else. He preferred to pop it himself, so I plunked the can down next to him.

I plopped down next to him, too, concentrating my hardest on not telling him about the cake Mom had hidden above the fridge. She wanted it to be a surprise but my mouth definitely didn't.

Larry raised his eyebrows, which were so thick and heavy that they took the attention off his crooked nose. "Forgetting something?"

For a second, I didn't know what he meant, but then I jumped up and got one of the fancy beer glasses Mom had found at the Salvation Army. It was an entire set of eight, and since one had a chip out of the rim, she got them for half price. She was the best at stuff like that. Every Sunday, she took ten dollars and went yard saleing. She didn't always spend it all because she didn't want to end up with just any old crud (she used a different word), but when she found something good, she always bargained the price down to practically nothing.

When I handed Larry the glass, there was a tiny wrinkle between his eyebrows. Mom tensed, her knuckles turning white as she clutched his plate at the stove. I held my breath, waiting to see if he would make it into a big deal that I'd forgotten the glass in the first place. He poured the beer, let it fizzle, and then took a long, thirsty swig. "Nectar of the gods," he said.

I let out a silent puff of air and sank into my chair. Mom's shoulders loosened. She dished food onto Larry's plate and set it in front of him. "Your favorite," she said, even though she'd told him that when he walked in the door.

A pile of grilled onions drowned a shriveled piece of liver, which Larry called a "super food." I wasn't a huge fan of meat on the best of days and especially not when it came to liver. I did my best not to wrinkle my nose, but I must not have done a very good job.

"You got a problem?" Larry asked.

"Just an itch." I reached up and scratched my nose.

Mom set a plate in front of me, and I worked to keep my face blank as I cut into the liver and mixed it with a cloud of fluffy potatoes. She knew how to make them perfectly, so they weren't lumpy or gray, and they almost masked the texture of the liver as it went down. Almost.

I got to the last bite, but I'd calculated wrong. I was out of potatoes, and only a single chunk of liver stared up at me. Larry stared at me, too, so I speared the meat with my fork and stuck it in my mouth, along with a swig of water that I used to wash it down.

The taste was unbearably gamy and the grainy texture even worse, but it was a small price to pay to get to dessert. The last time we had cake was my birthday all the way back in November, right after Mom met Larry. Even though we hadn't moved out here yet, and we barely knew him, he insisted Mom make carrot cake. Apparently he thought chocolate cake was too much sugar for a kid.

Larry took his time eating. If I didn't know better, I'd have thought he was doing it because he knew how eager I was for dessert. That couldn't be, because he didn't know about the cake. Unless maybe he smelled it when he walked in the door, but then why didn't he say something?

He finally slid his plate away and pushed back his chair. That was my cue. I jumped up and cleared the table. I didn't need him reminding me that we didn't have a garbage disposal and food going down the drain would clog the pipes, so I carefully scraped the plates into the trash before washing them in the sink.

While I worked, Larry complained about his day. He hated his job, and I couldn't say that I blamed him. His boss was a real piece of work. He only let Larry take breaks at scheduled times, and the guy rode him if he came in even a minute late. The good news was that once Larry's back stopped acting up and he returned to the ring, he wouldn't need to work at the mine anymore. When that happened, he planned to kiss his job goodbye. He said we'd kiss this trailer goodbye, too.

We'd move to the other side of town, where there were no trailers, and all the houses were big and brick and had lawns and garages (with enough room for two cars!), and there were sidewalks, and kids rode their bikes up and down the streets. He said I could trade the blow-up raft I slept in for a bunk bed, and we could think about getting a dog. (Mom wouldn't let me get so much as a goldfish before then—she said she had enough mouths to feed.)

But a fancy house wasn't the biggest reason I couldn't wait for him to start boxing again. Once he was back in the ring, he'd be happy. And then maybe he'd go back to the guy he was when Mom first met him—the guy who took her dancing and held her hand and treated her like a queen. In the meantime, I figured it was my job to stay on his good side—to make sure I never gave him a reason to blow up.

Finally, the dishes were done. I'd wiped out the sink and was folding the dish towel when a movement in the window caught my eye. A large, lanky coyote with fur the color of a burned biscuit disappeared around the back of the empty trailer across our dirt yard.

My breath caught. Larry said coyotes were all over the place out here, but I'd never actually seen one. According to my favorite book, a field guide on Wyoming animals, coyotes were masters of stealth. They could even live right in the middle of a big city without anyone knowing they were there. I stood on my tippy-toes, hoping to catch another glimpse, but the dry pasture beyond our trailer was empty.

"You about done over there?" Mom asked, breaking into my thoughts.

I lowered my heels and hung the dish towel over the edge of the sink with the tags hidden so it didn't look sloppy. "I'm finished."

My mouth watered as I eyed the cake. "Is it time?"

"Time for what?" Larry said, but his gaze slid to the top of the fridge. I was so excited for the cake, I didn't even care that he'd figured out the surprise. After a last glance out the window, I set out fresh plates while Mom grabbed the cake. It didn't say Happy Birthday or have decorations like the fancy ones from the grocery store, but she'd done a real nice job smoothing out the cream cheese–honey frosting, so it looked almost as good.

"Happy birthday to you," she sang, and I joined in. There weren't any candles for him to blow out, but Larry rubbed his hands together like he was looking forward to the cake as much as I was.

I handed him a knife. He cut me and Mom small slices and himself a giant slab, and we all dug in. I almost had the first bite in my mouth when I noticed that Larry was chewing with a strange expression on his face.

"What kind of crap is this?" he asked.

Mom laughed nervously. "I made it with carob and honey so it wouldn't ruin your diet."

Uh-oh.

Mom rushed to fix her mistake but tripped on her own tongue. "I mean—not that I'm saying you're—"

Larry dropped his fork. It clattered on his plate. "My *diet*?" he said. "You saying I need to be on a *diet*?"

When animals get scared, they have one of three responses: freeze, fight, or flight. Right now, I wanted nothing more than to run to my room. But it was like someone had poured cement inside me, and I couldn't move. The cement was spreading through my chest, making it so I could hardly breathe.

"No," Mom said. "Not at all. Only that I know how important it is for you to eat healthy to get back in the ring. I thought . . ."

"You thought?" he sneered. "It seems to me the problem is that you didn't think at all."

"I'm sorry," Mom said, wringing her hands.

"Let me tell you who's sorry. *I'm* sorry. Sorry that I'm stuck with someone who doesn't even know how to make a simple cake."

I cringed as he picked up his plate and dumped his slice back in the pan.

"You know what else I'm sorry about? I'm sorry you think I'm too fat to enjoy a nice slice of actual cake on my birthday. That me and my job aren't enough for you and your snivel-nosed daughter. I should have known that you were only in this for the money."

"That's not true." Mom's eyes filled with tears. Larry's belly had started to hang a little over his belt recently, but his thick arms were pure muscle, and no one would ever call him fat. As to wanting his money, well, Mom wasn't like that.

My eyes filled with tears, too.

But he wasn't done. "You want to know what I think of *you*?"

Mom pressed her lips together and looked down at her hands.

Larry pushed back his chair and stood up.

I tensed. This was it. His anger had been getting bigger and bigger lately, and it seemed only a matter of time before he snapped and hit Mom.

He grabbed the entire pan of cake, crossed the room in two giant steps, and dumped it into the sink. He wiped his hands on the dish towel and threw it on top of the pan. "That's what I think of you and your lousy cake."

He stormed down the hallway and slammed their bedroom door.

I looked from the piece of cake on my fork to the sadness on Mom's face. I wanted to say something to make her feel better, but all I could think of was how he shouldn't have dumped the cake in the sink because we didn't have a garbage disposal, and the last thing we needed was clogged pipes.

CHAPTER TWO

I set my fork down without taking the bite. If Larry found out I ate the cake he'd rejected, he might take it as a personal insult.

I picked at the peeling bits of skin around my nonexistent nails. A particularly large chunk of dried skin on my thumb caught my attention. I lifted my hand to my mouth and ripped at the skin with my teeth. It burned a little as I tore it away, but it was a good kind of burn—it matched the burning that was happening inside my chest.

Mom rubbed her temples and then nodded at my plate. "No sense in it going to waste."

I stared at the plate and then down the hall, where the *thwap, thwap, thwap* of Larry hitting his punching bag sounded.

Mom's hand shook as she picked up her fork. "Go on," she said. "He'll be in there for a while."

A small war happened inside me, like Mom and Larry were playing tug-of-war with my guts. I wanted Mom to be happy, and the best way to do that was to keep Larry happy. But my mouth flooded at the thought of chocolate, and I couldn't hold out any more. I raised my fork.

The cake was . . . not what I'd expected. It wasn't liver and onions bad, but it wasn't chocolate cake good, either. It was more like a chocolate cake that was made partially of mud and missing most of the sugar.

I tried not to make a face as I chewed. There had to be a way to get out of eating the rest, but I didn't want to hurt Mom's feelings, even if this whole thing was her fault. The carob and honey had cost more than plain old chocolate and sugar. She should have done what she was supposed to and made a normal cake, or better yet, bought one at the grocery store.

Why couldn't she be one of those mothers who went to college and got a big-deal job telling other people what to do so we could live in an air-conditioned house and have fancy cakes like everyone else?

Because she'd never been much of one for doing what everyone else did.

She actually had a scholarship to go to college after high school, but instead she moved out East somewhere and worked as a tour guide taking people white-water rafting. Then she got pregnant with me, and my father disappeared. She'd moved back here and struggled to keep us afloat ever since.

My chin dropped as guilt weighed me down. Mom was

doing the best she could. Besides, *she* wasn't the problem.

Across the table, Mom made a strange noise. I didn't want to make eye contact because I was afraid she'd know how much I hated the cake. I peeked out of the corner of my eye.

Mom wrinkled her nose. She couldn't stand the cake, either.

My lips turned up as I fought a grin.

She spat out her bite on the plate in front of her, and I did the same.

"Well," she said. "That was a fail, wasn't it?"

Suddenly Mom and I broke out in giant belly laughs even though neither one of us was sure exactly why. When we were done laughing, Mom reached over and grabbed my hand. Her hands were thin and veiny, but soft. She ran her pointer finger over my palm, tracing the lines like she was trying to read my future.

Thwap, thwap, thwap. The muffled sound of Larry's punches filled the air.

"He didn't mean it, you know," she said, without looking at me.

I didn't know how to respond, so I didn't say anything.

She continued. "Once his back is healed and he can get back in the ring, things will be better."

"When will that be?" We'd moved into Larry's trailer right after school got out. It started again on Monday, and Larry's back didn't seem any better now than it had then.

"These things take time." Mom obviously didn't want me to ask any more questions. She dropped my hand, and her voice changed to one that was bright and happy. "Tomorrow is yard saleing. Want to come?"

I was tempted. I'd been trapped out here all summer. We only left this place when we drove into town for groceries or to do laundry or yard saleing. That rarely happened because The Miracle, a beat-up Willys Jeep, had finally given up. Larry refused to fix it, so Mom had been forced to quit her job, and now we had to borrow his truck to go anywhere.

But the last time I went yard saleing with Mom was a total disaster. We'd left at 7:15 because the sales began at 8:00, and even though it was only a fifteen-minute drive to town, Mom always insisted on starting early so that we could get to the good stuff before all the vultures.

The morning had started out fine. Right away, Mom had scored a set of brand-new pot holders for only twenty-five cents. The slogan on them said World's Best Teacher, which I thought was kind of weird since Mom's not a teacher, but she said she didn't need her potholders to make sense, she needed them to protect her hands.

After that, we showed up at a brick house so big it was practically a mansion. Tables were set up all over the place, and I was barely out of the car when I saw that the sale was sponsored by the local Girl Scout troop to raise money for a trip to Disneyland.

I tried to get back in the car, but by then Mom had spotted a long rack of girls' clothes and called out, "Come on over, Fud, we've hit the jackpot."

A group of girls stepped from behind the racks and started giggling.

Not just any girls. Ava Benson and her crew. The coolest girls in school. Girls who now knew their castoffs were my jackpot.

Mom was still waiting for my answer about yard saleing tomorrow.

"I think I'll stick around here." I hated the disappointment on her face, so I excused myself to get ready for bed.

The yelling started almost as soon as I climbed into my raft. Mom apologized again and again for the cake, but Larry moved from that to how long it'd been since she'd changed the sheets and how she must be trying to get him fired because if he didn't have a comfortable bed to get a decent night's sleep, he'd end up late for work.

I curled up in a ball and covered my ears. When that didn't work, I squeezed my eyes shut and pictured the coyote I'd seen earlier. Lucky thing—it could do whatever it wanted. Go wherever it wanted.

As the yelling from the front of the trailer continued, I concentrated on blocking out their harsh words, on the darkness behind my eyelids, on existing somewhere outside of this small trailer. I was only vaguely aware of my arms growing long, of a thick layer of protective fur sprouting to cover my body. Of leaving the trailer on all fours, slinking through the shadowed kitchen so Mom and Larry didn't notice my exit.

Outside, Larry's angry voice cut through the trailer's thin walls, bringing me fully into a body that felt at once new and yet strangely comfortable. I sprang into action. Racing toward the bluff, my paws pounded the earth as hot wind propelled me across the prairie. Stars twinkled overhead, bathing tumbleweeds and the occasional tree in a soft glow.

I raised my snout and howled at the quarter moon. I was free. And strong. So strong. I ran for hours. For miles. My powerful haunches and long legs propelled me over windswept hills and sharp ridges, through small valleys and across the wide-open plains. The pleasant buzz of cicadas filled an otherwise silent night.

A den came into view, a small hole dug in the side of a gulley. The familiar scent of a pack enveloped me as I crawled into the inky blackness and nestled among a tangle of sprawled limbs. A pup squirmed and licked my muzzle. My body grew heavy and my mind fuzzy as sleep wrapped its arms around me.

The next morning, I wiggled my toes, vaguely disappointed by my human form, then laughed at myself. It wasn't as if people could turn into animals. The less time

I spent dreaming about things that would never happen, the better I'd be able to deal with the things that did.

I dragged myself out of bed. Larry's bad mood had vanished, but I didn't want to take any chances on it returning, so I left the trailer the same time as Mom. I sat on the steps as the faded-blue truck sputtered and roared to life. It needed a new muffler, but Larry wouldn't buy one. Mufflers were expensive, and as soon as he won his first big fight, he was going to trade the whole truck for a shiny new one anyway.

The truck crept down our gravel road and turned onto the highway. As it disappeared in the distance, I peeled myself from the already hot metal stairs and wandered to the back of the trailer.

I scanned the horizon, searching for the coyote I'd seen the evening before. Most people thought they were nocturnal, but that was only because coyotes were smart enough to stay hidden when they lived in crowded areas. Out here, they were free to hunt whenever they wanted.

Off in the distance, a bluff jutted up from the ground, making it feel like we were in a bit of a valley. A flat, nothing-filled valley. The whole state used to be under glaciers. When those melted, it was an ocean. I tried to imagine being underwater with sharks swimming around, but it was hard. There was pretty much nothing but dirt, sagebrush, and sun-crisped prairie grass as far as the eye could see—unless you counted the piles of junk scattered around Larry's property, which I didn't.

There were no signs of the coyote, so I rummaged around Larry's piles of wrecked cars, an old-fashioned washing machine with a crank handle, and barrels of who-knows-what.

I came across a poker that I'd found earlier in the summer. It was a long metal stick with prongs at the end, like something I imagined could be used for grilling marshmallows over a campfire. I climbed through the barbed-wire fence separating Larry's property from what must have been a pasture at some point because it was filled with dried-out bison chips. (Most people called them buffalo, but I knew better. Buffalo were only in Africa and Asia.)

I used the poker to flip over the chips. They looked exactly like you might expect on top—like flat, dried-out pieces of poop—but underneath was a whole different world. There were usually beetles and crickets and worms, but sometimes I got lucky and found a toad. Once, I even found a baby gopher snake, which I thought was a rattler until I noticed its more rounded head.

A small part of me felt bad for messing up their homes, but I kind of liked doing it, too. It was like the movie *Horton Hears a Who!*, only instead of being one of the helpless townspeople, I was actually in charge of what happened.

Playing with poop was probably weird, but I didn't

touch it or anything. Besides, it was important practice for becoming a wildlife biologist someday, and I always put it back when I was done. What else was I supposed to do, stuck out here by myself?

A tingling feeling crawled up my spine. My head popped up, and I searched the horizon. At first I didn't see anything, but then my eyes adjusted to the dull landscape. A coyote stood on top of the bluff, staring right at me.

My skin prickled. I didn't know if it was the one from last night or why I was suddenly seeing them everywhere. I wished I could see this coyote up close. They apparently had gold eyes, but I couldn't quite imagine that. If only I had binoculars. I'd asked for a pair last Christmas, but I'd gotten a small pillow instead (which was a whole lot better than the rolled-up sweatshirt I'd been using).

I held still, hoping the coyote would decide that I wasn't a threat and let me watch it hunt. After a long pause, it turned and disappeared over the ridge. I was tempted to follow, but I stayed put. Attacks on humans were rare, but they were still wild animals, and I had no interest in becoming a coyote snack.

I returned to the trailer and sank down on the stairs, trying to figure out what to do next.

I was picking a scab on my knee when a U-Haul appeared on the highway. Instead of driving by, the truck slowed down and put on a blinker.

My heart sped up, like the time I flipped over a bison chip and found the snake staring up at me. Could this be for real? The only other trailer out here had been empty all summer. There'd been some workers coming and going over the last few weeks, but Mom said not to get my hopes up—they were probably there for maintenance.

Still, I'd spent a little time daydreaming about what kind of family might move in. It'd be big, with enough kids to play softball out in the field or hide-and-seek around the junk piles. I never really thought it'd happen.

By now, the U-Haul had lumbered down the gravel road and was backing into the empty trailer's driveway, filling the air with a high-pitched beeping that made me want to cover my ears.

I was curious about who was inside, but I didn't want to seem like I didn't have anything better to do than rush over to see what was going on. I wandered toward the rusted-out tractor parked on the other side of the gravel road.

The tractor had giant wheels and a big, old-fashioned bucket seat that I could sit in and pretend to drive. I scampered up and gripped the wheel, trying to see inside the U-Haul without making it obvious that I was looking.

Of course the stupid sun glinted against the U-Haul's window, hiding the inside from my view. The door opened, and a woman wearing cutoffs and a T-shirt climbed out. She wasn't young, but she wasn't super old, either. Her white skin was tan and her shoulder-length hair was streaked blue. For a second, I thought she was the only person in the cab, but then the passenger door opened and a kid climbed out.

My heart started hammering again, this time harder than before. It was a girl, a younger version of the lady, only her blond hair was pulled back in a sleek ponytail. She looked to be about my age. At first, I could hardly believe my luck. Then my throat dried up like a ten-year-old bison chip.

This girl wasn't dressed the same as the woman I assumed was her mom. She was wearing a black-and-white polka-dot romper (A romper! What, did she think she was a movie star or something?) with a V-neck and a big bow tied at the waist. Instead of sneakers, she wore flip-flops with jewels that glinted in the sun, and she looked identical to the pack of girls who followed Ava Benson around school. They mocked everyone who couldn't afford to shop at malls and get their hair done at fancy salons and made up stupid nicknames for them like Fud-the-Dud and Elmer Fudd.

The girl flipped her ponytail. I groaned. What rotten luck—having a neighbor who was one of *those* girls was worse than not having any neighbor at all.

CHAPTER THREE

I hopped off the tractor and slinked toward Larry's trailer, hoping the girl would be too busy unloading to notice me. I'd almost made it when footsteps sounded off to my side. I pretended I didn't hear them and sped up, but just before I got to the stairs, she spoke.

"Hey, you must be my new neighbor."

I stopped and closed my eyes, trying to pull myself together like I'd seen Mom do a million times. Reluctantly, I turned to face her. "Yeah, so what?"

The girl's eyes widened, but then she cracked a smile and pressed forward. "So my name is Everleigh, but my friends call me Leigh, and if we're going to be neighbors we should definitely be friends, don't you think?"

For a second, I felt as though I'd won the lottery. Then I remembered who she was—who *I* was. Usually these girls had some sort of radar that could pick out kids like me from a million miles away. I waited for her to take a good, long look. To see the too-small T-shirt I'd pulled on from yesterday and my toe sticking out of my scruffy sneakers. My frizzy hair and dirty hands.

When I felt certain that she'd had enough time, I said, "I'm not looking for any new friends right now."

She sagged, and I thought maybe she'd finally gotten the message, but then she brightened. "Okay, well, we don't have to be friends, but since we're neighbors, we should at least be acquaintances. I've never ridden a school bus. We should sit together. What's your name, anyway?"

My brain was buzzing because I'd never met someone who talked so much but also because if I heard her right, she'd asked if I wanted to sit with her on the bus.

She stared at me with wide eyes, waiting for an answer. I meant to say that I always sat alone, but when I opened my mouth, the word *yes* came out.

She giggled. "Your name is yes?"

Her giggle wasn't mean, but heat started building in my toes and filled me up until even my cheeks turned red. If this was how hard it was to have friends, or *acquaintances*, I didn't want any part of it.

"My name is Fud." It was actually Felicity Ulyssa Dahlers, but everyone had called me Fud my whole life. Most of the time, I didn't mind. "Felicity" meant happiness, and every time I heard it, I thought of some girl running around smiling at everybody. So Fud was fine. Unless, of course, I was around Ava Benson and her pack of rats, in which case it wasn't fine at all.

I crossed my arms and stared at Leigh, daring her to laugh.

She cocked her head to the side. "Fud," she said, like she was tasting the word in her mouth. "I like it."

And then she did the weirdest thing: she bent over backwards and casually flipped her legs over her head, one after the other.

She was quite a bit shorter than me, but the muscles in her shoulders and arms reminded me of Larry. Pipes, he'd call them. She stood up and wiped the dust from her hands as if nothing had happened. "It reminds me of Fudgsicles, which are about my most favorite things in the world. I think that's a good sign, don't you? It must mean we're going to be great friends."

She hurried to correct herself. "I mean acquaintances. Anyway, I'm totally in the mood for a Fudgsicle; it's as hot as a dragon's butt out here. But we have a ton of unloading to do, and we don't have any groceries yet. As soon as we get to the store, I'm going to ask Mom to buy a box first thing."

She stopped talking and looked at me like I was supposed to say something, but I had no idea what. This girl reminded me of a friendly puppy, eager to play with anyone she met. She didn't seem to get that I was no puppy. I was more of a . . . what was I?

I pictured the coyote standing at the top of the bluff. It wouldn't have been hanging around if it wasn't part of a nearby pack. But not all coyotes had packs. Some of them traveled alone.

I opened my mouth to tell her I'd changed my mind about sharing seats when Larry's truck sputtered up the dirt road.

The truck turned into our driveway. "Your mom?" Leigh asked.

"Yep."

Mom killed the engine and joined us.

"What's going on over there?" She held up her hand to protect her eyes from the sun as she squinted at the U-Haul.

"We're moving in," Leigh said.

"I thought the last set of renters trashed the trailer so bad that the new landlord vowed not to let any more in?"

"We're not really renters. The landlord is my uncle. We're from Cheyenne, but my mom said living in the city was killing her creativity. She says art is like a garden—it needs fresh air and space to grow."

Mom and I stared at her.

"She's a photographer," Leigh said. "Her work is amazing. You'll have to come check it out once we're settled."

"Your mother will have plenty of space for her creativity out here," Mom said. "We like to keep to ourselves."

Now I stared at Mom, wondering if an alien had come down from another galaxy, sucked out her brain, and replaced it with a new one. My mom loved people. No matter where we lived before, she was always getting to know everyone. This lady standing in front of me saying she kept to herself was a total stranger.

"It was nice meeting you," Mom said. She glanced one last time at Leigh's trailer and then started toward the truck. "Fud, can you help me out?"

"Gotta go," I told Leigh, grateful for the chance to escape.

I bristled when she followed. The less she knew about me, the less she and Ava Benson would have to make fun of.

A basket of clean laundry took up the passenger seat. An enormous houseplant sat on the floor, bushy and tall enough that it brushed the ceiling. I groaned. Mom had a thing for houseplants. Which was fine, except she didn't exactly have a green thumb. In fact, she had the opposite of a green thumb. What would that be? The color wheel from art ran through my mind. A red thumb, maybe? Orange?

"Look at this beauty," Mom said.

I was looking, but I only saw the dry, crunchy plant it would become when she forgot to water it.

Mom beamed. "They wanted ten dollars for it, but I talked them down to eight."

That explained why she was home early—she'd blown through most of her ten-dollar budget on one stinking houseplant. A houseplant she'd never be able to keep alive.

At least she never gave up—I had to give her that much.

I was about to reach in and help when Mom whirled around, her eyes bright with excitement. Her hands were hiding behind her back. "Guess what else I got?"

I perked up.

There were always lemonade stands set up by kids trying to make money off the yard sale traffic. Every once in a while, Mom splurged. She obviously wasn't hiding a cup of lemonade behind her back, but I could practically taste a chocolate chip cookie. Or peanut butter or even raisin. Anything but molasses—there should be a law against ruining cookies like that.

Mom pulled her hands from behind her back and offered me a stuffed elephant. A bright pink elephant with a shiny gold crown on its head.

If the truck had been moving, I would have thrown myself under it and let it run me over. I had a whole collection of stuffed animals before we moved out here, but Larry said they were for babies and made me get rid of them. Even though I'd been sad, I'd realized he was right. I was going into seventh grade—I couldn't keep stuffed animals all over my room.

I glanced at Leigh, sure that this was it—the moment she realized what a loser her new neighbor was and made some excuse to slink away and never talk to me again.

"Oh my gosh, it's so cute!" she squealed.

Mom handed me the elephant.

"I love stuffed animals. I have an entire collection. Once my bedroom is unpacked, you have to come over and help me organize them. I can never decide how to do it."

"Species and then color," I said automatically.

"Perfect." She did a cartwheel. "We're going to have so much fun together."

My heart swelled up bigger than a balloon. Maybe Leigh wasn't an Ava Benson kind of girl after all.

She clapped her hands and spun toward me. "I have the best idea!"

Her face was all lit up like she'd just invented Christmas. She reached in her pocket and pulled out a bright-yellow flyer. "I found this at the gas station when we stopped. If we both apply, maybe we can do it together!"

"What is it?"

"Miss Tween Black Gold! It's open to anyone aged ten to thirteen."

The balloon in my chest didn't just shrivel—it flat out popped. Miss Tween Black Gold was a beauty pageant sponsored by Powder River Coal. The pageants on television were full of beautiful girls wearing skimpy swimsuits and fancy dresses and talking about ending gun violence and saving the world or whatever.

Mom's expression was bemused, like she couldn't imagine me in a pageant. I couldn't imagine me in a pageant, either.

I crossed my arms over my chest. "I have to go."

"Okay, but what about the pageant?"

"Beauty pageants stink." I whirled around and marched toward the trailer, angry at myself for having let my guard down.

"Fud, get back here right now," Mom called.

I thought she was going to make me apologize, but when I got back to the truck, she only pointed at the plant and said, "Help me get this inside."

"I can help, too," Leigh said.

"We've got it." *Jeez*. This girl really was a puppy. But the thing about puppies was that they eventually turned into dogs. And dogs required an alpha—a leader to keep them in line.

The last thing I needed was her acting like we were friends now, only to get to school on Monday and be snapped up by Ava Benson. They'd be perfect for each other with their shiny hair and pageant babble. Pretty soon, Leigh would pretend she didn't know me and join in with the snickers that followed me when I walked down the hall wearing a purple and pink backpack from three years ago.

Leigh glanced at her trailer. Her mom had opened the back of the U-Haul and was busy putting together a ramp. "Okay," she said brightly. "I should get to work anyway. My uncle will be here soon to help us unload. It was awfully nice to meet you—"

"I'm Crystal," Mom said. "I didn't catch your name."

"I'm Leigh and my mom over there is Catherine, but she goes by Click."

"Click?" Mom furrowed her brows.

"You know, like a camera?" Leigh mimed holding a camera up to her face and pressing the button.

"Well, Leigh, thanks for dropping by," Mom said.

"Oh, it's no problem." Leigh turned to me. "In case we don't see each other tomorrow, the bus leaves at 7:15 on Monday. Knock on my door, and we can walk to the stop together."

She skipped off without waiting for a response.

"Seems like a nice girl," Mom said.

I didn't respond. Mom thought the same thing about Larry when she first met him. Actually, that wasn't fair. He *was* nicer when we met him. He even brought Mom flowers on their first few dates. Things didn't really change until we moved in, which was about the same time the doctors told him he wouldn't be getting back into the ring anytime soon.

That first night, we'd had vegetable soup for dinner, and I'd picked out the onions like I always did. Before I even knew what was happening, I was over his knee. I'd never been spanked before, and I thought for sure we'd leave in a hurry, but Mom just said onions were good for me, and that was that.

I went around to the driver's side of the truck, climbed in, and scooted the plant into Mom's arms.

A coyote yipped in the distance. According to my field guide, they had several vocalizations. Unfortunately, it didn't say anything about what the different sounds meant. I made a mental note to look it up once our laptops were issued at school.

In the meantime, I was glad Leigh had made like the coyote I'd spotted earlier and disappeared.

The next day, I kept to the trailer because I didn't want to take any chances on being cornered by Leigh again. Larry was off doing whatever it was he did when he left the trailer on a Sunday morning. That was fine with me. With him gone, I didn't have to worry about getting yelled at for every little thing I did.

I spent the day working on a crossword puzzle and stressing about school. Starting seventh grade on my own would have been bad enough, but now I had fancy-pants Leigh to deal with, too. I was making bets with myself about how fast Ava Benson would suck her into the cool crowd (thirty seconds, tops) when a loud rumbling came from outside the trailer. I ran to the window.

An enormous truck—as big as a garbage truck but with a flatbed—was backing into our driveway. But that wasn't the weirdest thing. The weirdest thing was the rusted-out boat strapped to the back. It was gigantic—the kind of fishing boat you see out on the ocean in movies. *What the heck?*

I ran outside.

Larry jumped out of the cab and grinned. "What do you think?"

"What is it?"

The grin fell off his face. "What do you mean 'what is it'—it's a boat."

"I can see that," I said, not meaning to be sassy but sounding a bit like it anyway. "But what's it for?"

"It's a houseboat," Larry said. "Or it will be when I'm done with it."

The boat, which was tipped on its side, had a pointed bottom, steep walls, and no roof.

"Once we get rid of all this rust and clean it up, I'll build a cabin with a couple of berths, a head, and a galley. It'll have everything we need to survive."

I didn't know what a berth, head, or galley was, but the last part, I got. "You mean we're going to live on it?"

Larry rubbed his hands together. "That's the plan."

He might as well have dropped an anchor down my throat because something big and hard traveled down my chest and landed in my stomach.

Mom opened the trailer door and rubbed her eyes. "What's going on?"

Larry's chest puffed up so huge I thought it might pop. "Isn't she a beauty?"

Mom's mouth opened and then shut. I could tell she thought this was some kind of trap where the wrong response would set Larry off.

"Looks like she could use some work," she said carefully.

Larry dismissed her with a wave of his hand. "Nothing some TLC won't fix."

Mom climbed down the stairs, pulling the robe she hadn't bothered to change out of tight around her. "How much did this bad boy cost us?"

A muscle bulged in Larry's jaw. "Not a cent."

"Somebody gave you a boat for free? What, they handed it to you out of the goodness of their heart?" She tried to keep her voice light and teasing, but there was a tiny bite in her question.

"No, someone didn't give it to me for free," Larry mocked. "As it happens, I traded my ring for her."

"Your Great Plains Golden Ring?" Mom's eyes opened wide—she looked about as shocked as I felt.

Larry's ring was his pride and joy. Winning Great Plains had been his big break. If he hadn't hurt his back, he would have gone on to fight at Nationals and from there, gone pro. That was still his plan, so I couldn't believe he'd traded his ring for a boat. Apparently, neither could Mom.

"You love that ring—what were you thinking?"

Larry pulled himself up tall and clenched his fists.

Uh-oh.

"I was *thinking* that I'd like to do something nice for my family. That maybe we deserved more than being stuck here for the rest of our lives. That we could do a little traveling. You got a problem with that?"

"Sounds expensive," Mom said. "You know that ring could have bought me a new car. Or filled our fridge for a year."

Double uh-oh. Instead of waiting around for Larry's response, I raced into the trailer and down the hall, taking refuge in my room. An ocean-sized typhoon raged inside of me, making my skin flushed and clammy.

On one hand, living on a boat sounded exciting. And glamorous. I pictured the yachts I sometimes saw on television, with fancy leather seats and butlers serving drinks. On the other hand, there were only three lakes around here. When we were "glamping," which is what Mom called it when she got a toothache and had to use her paycheck to see a dentist instead of paying rent and we ended up living out of The Miracle, we used to clean up at their public beaches. None of the lakes were big enough for a boat like this.

I flopped into my raft and ran a finger along the yellow plastic. Larry had mentioned traveling. Did he mean to take us to the ocean?

I imagined us cruising from one destination to the next: Australia, the Caribbean, South America—places I'd always wanted to see. But not like this. Out on the ocean, the boat would turn into a giant floating prison. One with two human punching bags.

Apparently, Mom agreed, because she and Larry were really going at it. They'd moved their fight inside, and their shouting practically shook the walls. I tried to reassure myself she wouldn't let the boat thing happen, but it was hard to focus on that when I was listening for the sound of bones breaking, or worse, sudden silence. Larry loved to point out that there were plenty of places out here where a body would never be found.

Around and around they went. I snatched up the book next to my bed and smoothed a hand over the scuffed cover. *Field Guide: A Survey of Wyoming Wildlife* had been my grandma's. She'd loved animals, and my favorite stories were the ones Mom told about all the different critters Grandma had rescued over the years. I never met her, but this book, already worn from years of use before it became mine, made me think we would have gone together like black bears and berries.

"Don't you tell me what to do," Larry yelled. Something crashed against the wall.

I startled, then pressed the guide against my chest. Stretching out on my back, I forced my body to relax, releasing the tension in my jaw, my shoulders, and my arms. The book rose and fell as I sucked in deep, even breaths. *In. Out. In. Out.*

Mom hollered something I couldn't catch.

In. Out. In. Out.

Larry hollered back.

I continued breathing, sinking ever deeper into a place where I was safe, where the sounds of their battle couldn't reach me.

A coyote howled a summons. The call reverberated inside me, refusing to be ignored. My body quivered like a plucked guitar string, filling me with a longing so intense that I found myself on four paws, racing across the prairie with my tail streaming behind me. Hot wind pushed back my fur. Scents filled my nose. The smell of a nearby mouse. Sagebrush. A hint of exhaust and coffee. My pack.

I greeted the alpha female with a submissive whine. She nodded and then went back to licking her fur, a sandy color marked by a distinctive black patch near her tail. I wrestled with her milk-scented pups, who nipped and yipped joyfully as they darted around me.

Warm sun beat down on my back. Eventually, we grew weary and settled down for a mid-afternoon nap, nestled among the roots of a lonely tree. The pups pressed up against me, squirming and then settling. I marveled at the warmth from their small bodies, the rise and fall of their bellies as they pulled in slow, gentle breaths.

"Get your hands off me," Mom yelled, drawing me back to the trailer, back to my own body. The calm I'd felt only moments before disappeared. My muscles clenched. As if things weren't bad enough, my legs ached. I shifted on the raft, but the throbbing pain deep in my bones continued. Great. A growth spurt was the last thing I needed right now.

If only I could return to the comfort of my pack.

CHAPTER FOUR

Larry's truck roared to life, jolting me awake. My stomach churned like it was filled with a mess of scorpions, drowning out the pain in my legs. Today was the first day of seventh grade.

I crawled out of the raft. Despite the late summer heat, shorts weren't allowed in school. I tugged on a pair of jeans Mom had picked up at a yard sale earlier in the summer. The only other pair I owned had a hole in the knee, so these would have to do. After brushing my teeth and corralling my curls into the same ponytail I wore every day, I joined Mom in the kitchen.

She hunched over a bowl at the table, which had three chairs now instead of four. That answered my question about the crash I'd heard last night.

"Oatmeal's on the stove," she said. "There's still a bit of honey left. Make sure you add some peanut butter for protein."

After I fixed my bowl, I sank down next to Mom, who stirred her own oatmeal without taking a bite.

"So," I said.

"So what?"

"What'd you decide about the boat?"

She set down her spoon. "What do you mean, what did I *decide*?"

"Did you tell Larry it was a no go?"

Mom's head lifted. Her right eye was swollen nearly shut and circled by a dark bruise.

I gasped. "He *hit* you?"

"It was an accident. He apologized." She bent her head again, covering her cheek with her hair.

I stabbed my spoon into my oatmeal and left it standing straight up. I'd been living in almost constant fear that Larry would snap and really hurt Mom. Now he had, and I couldn't believe she was acting as if it was all a big mistake. "You told him we can't live on a boat, right?"

"You don't understand." Her eyes drilled into me, pleading with me to get on board. "The boat is going to be a new beginning for him. For all of us. Once we get out of here, things will be different."

"What about boxing? Larry will be back in the ring soon. That's supposed to be our new beginning."

Mom shook her head.

"But that's always been the plan." I fought the panic pressing against my ribs. "He'll start boxing again, and then he'll be able to quit his job, and there will be more money, and we'll—"

"Boxing is over," Mom said. "Another back injury and he'd end up paralyzed. The doctor said he's done for good."

"Since when?"

"Apparently he's known for a few weeks, but he only told me yesterday." She stirred her oatmeal again.

I sat back in my chair, stunned. Boxing was Larry's passion. His dream. If he didn't have that . . .

"We can't get on that boat with him." I grabbed Mom's free hand.

A tear slid down her face. "What do you want me to do?" she whispered.

When coyotes mated, it was for life. But Mom wasn't a coyote. "Let's leave. Get your old job back. We'll rent a place."

She pulled her hand away and wiped her face. "Fud, get real. I don't have a car. Or any money. If we leave Larry, we're back on the streets. Maybe for good."

"There must be something we can do."

"There is," Mom said. The way she said it made it clear I wasn't going to like whatever was coming.

My throat ached like I'd swallowed a lump of dry peanut butter. "What?"

"Finish your oatmeal and get your butt out to the bus before you miss your first day of school."

I shoved my oatmeal away. The ache in my legs had returned, but the fact that I was apparently on my way to becoming a giraffe didn't seem important now. "What about you? What about your eye?"

"No one ever died from a black eye," she said. "Now get going."

She was done with this conversation. But I wasn't—not by a long shot. If we needed money to escape Larry, I'd find a way to get it.

A trickle of sweat ran down the back of my knees as I stormed toward the bus.

"Fud!"

I groaned and turned around in time to see Leigh spring from her doorway and land lightly on the ground. She sprinted toward me, brushing her loose hair from her face. Her skirt bunched at the waist, and a short-sleeved shirt with silver threads woven through it sparkled in the sun. She had on a matching headband and wore the same glittery sandals from when I'd first seen her. Did she ever dress like she wasn't a supermodel?

"You didn't knock," she said, panting.

"Forgot."

She giggled. "How could you forget—you walked right by the trailer."

"My mind was on other things, okay?"

"Okay. Jeesh. You don't have to get snippy. You must not be much of a morning person. My mom isn't, either. I don't even try to talk to her until she's at least halfway through her coffee. Anyway, I'm glad I saw you walk by. I'm so nervous!"

I would probably have been nervous, too, if I didn't have bigger things on my mind. Like Mom sitting at home with a black eye. And how I was going to come up with a whole heap of money when I'd never earned a cent in my entire life.

"Back in Cheyenne, I walked," Leigh continued. "Riding the bus is new for me. I'm glad I have you to sit with, or I'd be a wreck right now."

I side-eyed her to see if she was serious.

"I hope we're in some of the same classes," she said. "Wait, you *are* in seventh grade, right?"

I nodded.

"Whew! I wasn't sure for a second. You look older, like you could be one of the eighth graders."

I flushed and crossed my arms over my chest.

"Anyway, I've never been to a new school before. I hope the kids like me. Are they nice? Please tell me they're nice."

She finally paused, waiting for an answer.

"I'm sure they'll like you."

"Thank you for saying that." She rested a hand on my arm.

The relief in her eyes surprised me. She was genuinely nervous, which didn't make one bit of sense. The question wasn't whether kids would like *her*, it was how fast she would drop me once she realized they didn't like *me*.

Luckily, I was saved from having to say anything by the bus roaring up the highway.

"Here it comes!" Leigh clapped her hands like we were kindergarteners.

The bus rumbled to a stop in front of us. The driver, a skinny white man with a string of red licorice hanging out of his mouth, opened the door. "Hop on," he said, flashing us a grin.

"After you," Leigh said, motioning for me to take the lead.

I climbed the stairs, grimacing at the peach air freshener dangling from the window. Larry always insisted Mom buy the peach jelly he liked for my peanut butter sandwiches instead of the strawberry jam I loved.

I slid into a seat. I wanted to plop my backpack next to me so there wouldn't be a place for Leigh, but I pulled it into my lap and tried to cover the stars I'd drawn all over it with a sharpie in fifth grade.

"Does the driver remind you of anyone?" Leigh asked, settling in next to me with a brand-new backpack balanced on her knees.

The driver had big orange hair and was wearing a short-sleeved shirt that had colorful lollipops printed all over it, like a real-life Ms. Frizzle from *The Magic School Bus*.

"Nope."

"He looks exactly like Ms. Frizzle!" She leaned over and whispered. "I bet we're not on our way to school. We're on our way to the bottom of the ocean, where we'll be swallowed by a whale, never to be seen again."

A drop of sweat slid down my neck. It was even hotter on the bus than it was outside.

"Will it be cooler at the bottom of the ocean?" I reached up to open a window.

Leigh giggled.

She chattered all the way to school, but I hardly listened. A nuclear bomb had been dropped over my entire life. I couldn't believe Larry would never box again. He'd been almost unbearable waiting to get back in the ring. Now that he'd started beating up on Mom, it didn't seem likely that he'd stop.

And being trapped with him on a boat—even if he suddenly became the nicest guy on the planet, and even if he managed to turn the heap of junk in our driveway into something livable—where would we get the money for groceries? And what about school and doctors and dentists and all those sorts of things?

The bus slowed and then turned onto the street in front of Powder River Middle School, a low, wide building that sprawled down the block.

"Come on," Leigh said, jumping from her seat. "I can't wait until we get our schedules. I hope we have some of the same classes."

I stepped off the bus and ran smack into Ava Benson, causing her to drop the compact mirror she'd been holding up to admire her own perfect face. She'd tanned over the summer and started wearing eyeliner, too. It winged out from her hazel eyes, making her look more like a college student than a seventh-grade girl.

"What the—" she said, bending to pick up her compact, which luckily hadn't shattered.

"Sorry," I muttered, determined to make a quick getaway.

Ava straightened and adjusted her short, tight miniskirt. Bright red toenails peeked out from a pair of sandals with straps that wrapped around her ankles. "Oh, it's you."

She skimmed me up and down, and her nose wrinkled slightly. Then her eyes brightened. "You're wearing something from your *jackpot*."

The group of girls around her laughed. Humiliation spread through my body, making me feel as hot and prickly as a cactus in the desert sun. As I rushed away, I heard her singing voice lilt, "*Cha-ching*. Jackpot!"

Their laughter followed me all the way to the front door of the school, where Leigh finally caught up.

"Who was that?" she asked, casting a glance back at Ava.

"Ava Benson and her crowd." The pain in my legs flared up again, making me wince. If only my body had picked another day for a massive growth spurt.

Leigh glanced behind us one more time. "They were probably goofing around," she said. "Now come on—show me where the auditorium is."

It was all I could do not to snort. Ava and I had gone to the same elementary school. When she found out Mom and I were glamping back in second grade, she told everyone I was homeless. And then she invited every single girl in our third-grade class to her birthday party. Every single girl except me.

I glanced over my shoulder. Tyler, who everyone said was the cutest boy in school, but I thought was obnoxious even if he did have big blue eyes and dimples, was smiling down at Ava. She latched onto his arm as if staking out her territory. *Good thing she isn't a coyote or she'd be marking him right now.* But not even the image of her peeing on his shoe could chase away my lousy mood.

"Come on," a teacher called over the excited first-day-of-school chatter. "Let's move it along, everyone."

I stomped toward the auditorium, wishing we really had been swallowed by a whale. Leigh thinking Ava was harmless only proved that sooner or later, she'd join the pack.

We didn't have any classes together, but sure enough, when the lunch bell rang, I spotted Leigh and Ava walking toward the cafeteria together.

They stopped at the water fountain to get a drink. I inched to the other side of the hallway, hoping to pass without notice.

"I already have my gown," Ava said, bending for a sip.

"Lucky!" Leigh squealed. "Mom said we had to get settled before we could start shopping."

I rolled my eyes. Of course they were talking about the pageant.

"I was runner-up last year," Ava said, smoothing her ponytail. "Everyone says I'll win this year for sure."

"What will you do with the prize money?" Leigh asked.

Prize money? I froze.

"Mom said fifteen hundred has to go into my college fund, but I can do what I want with the other five hundred."

Holy horned lizards! Two *thousand* dollars? Leigh must have felt my surprised stare drilling into her back, because she turned around.

"There you are, Fud!" she said. "I've been looking for you all morning!"

"She sits alone in the loser seats," Ava said, tugging on Leigh's elbow. "Come eat lunch with us."

"That's sweet of you to ask," Leigh said, completely ignoring Ava's mean comment. "But I already planned to sit with Fud."

This was news to me.

She clapped her hands together like she had a great idea. "Maybe we could all sit together. Fud, we were just talking about the pageant."

"Pageants aren't exactly Fud's thing," Ava said, twirling her hair around her finger.

She was right—pageants weren't my thing.

But I'd prance around onstage all day for two thousand smackeroos. Besides, I couldn't stand the smug look on Ava's face.

Before I could think better of it, I opened my mouth. "I wouldn't be so sure of that crown," I told Ava. "Because I plan to give you a run for your money."

Leigh squealed and threw her arms around my neck. "I'm so glad you changed your mind! We're going to have a blast!"

But it wasn't fun I was interested in. As I shrugged out of Leigh's grasp, I imagined handing Mom a thick wad of cash.

CHAPTER FIVE

Mr. Frizzle handed us Blow Pops as we got off the bus that afternoon. "You two have a blessed evening."

I said thank you, but I doubted there would be anything blessed about my evening. Leigh bounced all the way home, talking nonstop about the pageant, how much fun it would be if we were both chosen to participate, and how we could shop for dresses together. As we walked along the gravel road, I seriously considered sticking my Blow Pop in her eyeball just to shut her up.

About a million times I opened my mouth to tell her I'd changed my mind, and about a million times I clamped it shut again. If there was any chance that I could win a single cent of the prize money, then there was no choice.

Even if the thought of all that makeup, all those sequins, all those gossipy Ava-Benson-type girls—not to mention prancing around in a swimsuit—made me want to vomit. "I'm not wearing a bikini."

"Don't worry. There's no swimsuit competition."

At least that was one less thing I had to worry about.

"The pageant isn't until October sixteenth, but the application deadline is August thirty-first," Leigh said. "That gives us eight days, but we should turn ours in right away to be safe."

"What flavor is your Blow Pop?" I asked, hoping to change the subject.

"Watermelon!" Leigh said. "My favorite!" She unwrapped the sucker and slipped it in her mouth.

Operation Blow Pop for the win! I pulled the wrapper off mine and savored the sugary sour apple taste almost as much as the silence.

Leigh stopped at her driveway and pulled the sucker from her mouth. "Why don't you come over? We can do our applications together. Our place is a mess, but Mom won't care."

I groaned silently. This girl had a one-track mind. I searched for an excuse to get out of applying today. "I'm not sure, I'd have to ask—"

"Or we can go to your place," Leigh said.

"No!"

She raised an eyebrow.

We didn't have a computer, and I didn't want her to see Mom's face. "Your place is fine."

"Great," Leigh said. She did a funny little skip-jump. "Do you like barbeque chips?"

I loved barbeque chips, but I almost never got them. Mom said they were way too expensive for a bag that was mostly air. Leigh kept talking, but my head was spinning because we weren't even friends, and suddenly I was climbing the stairs to her trailer. "Wait," I said, "I'd better let Mom know where I'm at."

Not to mention the fact that I hadn't asked for permission to do the pageant yet.

"Text her from my place."

No way was I going to admit that Larry was the only one with a phone. "Her phone is broken," I said. "I'll be right back."

I walked to our trailer as slowly as possible, wishing there was a way to turn back time. I'd rewind to lunch and take back what I said about the pageant. No, I'd rewind to yesterday, before Larry brought home his boat. Actually, I'd probably rewind all the way to last fall, before Mom even met Larry. But that could be a double-edged sword. Even though we wouldn't need to get rid of him now if we'd never met him in the first place, we might be stuck living in The Miracle, or even worse.

It didn't matter. Instead of going backward in time, each step carried me forward. Around the boat, up the stairs, and into our trailer. My legs, which had ached all day, continued to hurt as I shut the door behind me. Mom was on the couch reading one of the zillion romance novels she'd taken to buying at yard sales. Larry refused to get a television because he thought it would rot our minds. Mom's long hair blocked her face, so I couldn't see if her eye was any better. I dropped my backpack on the floor.

She didn't glance up from the book's worn pages. "That time of day already?"

I wondered how long she'd been on the couch, but I figured asking would put her in a bad mood, which I couldn't afford right now.

She tucked her hair behind her ear, revealing her bruised eye.

I tried to sound casual. "Do you mind if I go over to Leigh's to apply for the pageant?"

She finally set down the book.

Her eye was still swollen, the skin stained violent shades of red and purple. If anything, it looked worse.

"I thought you said pageants were stupid?"

I shrugged, figuring my best bet was to act like it was no big deal. "Leigh made it sound kind of fun."

I told myself I was keeping the truth from her because I didn't want to get her hopes up about the prize money until I had it, but I was actually scared she'd say no if she knew the real reason.

She squinted at my pants. "Did you have another growth spurt when I wasn't looking?"

My brows knit together as I tried to follow the abrupt change of subject. I inspected my pants. My frown deepened. I would swear they were at least an inch shorter than when I'd put them on this morning. But that was impossible. Besides, I wasn't going to let Mom change the subject. "Is that a yes?"

She chewed on her lip like she always did when she was thinking hard. The movement made her wince, and she touched her bruise. "I don't know how I feel about you being in a pageant. They're kind of . . . old-fashioned, aren't they?"

"It's no big deal," I said. "Just something fun to do with Leigh. I probably won't get accepted anyway."

"How much is it going to cost?"

Leigh had mentioned an application processing fee on the bus. "It's five dollars to enter. There's no fee if you're selected to compete."

"Five dollars could buy an entire bag of rice."

"I can use the money I found at the Laundromat."

She rubbed her temples. "I don't know."

"Please, Mom!"

She let out a long, defeated sigh. Before she could change her mind, I yelled out a thanks and took off. I was halfway to Leigh's trailer before I realized what my victory meant. Now that I had Mom's permission, I had to actually enter the pageant. I'd walked myself straight into another double-edged sword.

Leigh pulled open the door before I reached it. "Come in," she said. "I got our snacks ready."

I'd hoped to get the registration over with quickly, but I'd make an exception for barbeque chips. I kicked off my shoes.

The living room and kitchen were all stacked with boxes, but it was obvious the carpet was new, and the walls had been freshly painted. A collection of leafy green plants sat in colorful pots under a window. A pile of flattened cardboard blocked the sink. Leigh's mother rummaged in a box sitting on a cool round table on the far side of the living room. The wooden top was ringed like it had been sliced from an enormous tree. She was an older version of Leigh, except she was wearing cut-off overalls and a tank top that showed off a tattoo of a bright orange goldfish in a bowl on her arm.

She smiled as she quit working and closed the space between us. I wiped my sweaty hands on my pants. In movies, kids called adults Mr. and Mrs. and shook their hands when they met. But this was real life, and I hadn't been to another kid's house since I was so little that nothing was expected of me except not writing my name in boogers on the bathroom wall (which I learned the hard way).

Turned out, I didn't have to worry about what to do, because she wrapped her arms around me and squeezed.

I shifted. It was awkward being hugged by a stranger, but her smell—cedar mixed with a hint of vanilla—made me want to melt into her arms and hug her back.

"Fud," she said, pulling away. "I'm Click. It's nice to meet you."

Mom was a stickler for manners—she said just because we weren't rich didn't mean we had to act poor—so I offered Click my hand to shake.

"I'm glad Leigh is going to have a friend out here," she said, clasping my hand in both of hers. "I was worried about her being all alone in the country."

I didn't want to burst her bubble by telling her that Leigh and I weren't really friends, so I kept my mouth shut.

"She tells me you two are going to do the pageant together."

She looked me up and down. Then she whistled and cupped my chin. "The camera must really love you."

Leigh rolled her eyes. "Mom loves anyone with great cheekbones."

I didn't know what cheekbones had to do with anything, but I made a mental note to check mine in the mirror later.

"Come on," Leigh said, picking up the tray she'd filled with snacks and leading me toward a room at the front of the trailer. In Larry's trailer, both bedrooms and the bathroom were in the back.

"Break a leg," Click called after us.

Leigh groaned. "Mom, that's only for the theater."

Her mother's laughter followed us into Leigh's

bedroom, which was like something straight out of a movie.

"Wow," I said, breathing in a bright floral scent. "Your room is great."

"Mom wanted me to feel settled before school started, so we spent all day yesterday putting it together."

It wasn't just that she had her own bathroom. She also had a real bed. Not any old bed—an enormous bed. With a headboard that had obviously once been a set of window shutters. It wasn't old and junky, though, it was painted purple and strung with fairy lights. It looked like one of those pieces of furniture that tried hard to seem regular but actually cost a million dollars.

"Mom and I made that," Leigh said. "We love to upcycle."

"Upcycle?"

"You know, take one thing and make it into something else."

I couldn't imagine taking a piece of junk and turning it into something cool. Unless my raft counted. But it probably didn't, since I hadn't changed it into anything else—I only pretended it was something it wasn't.

Leigh set the tray on the bed and flopped down next to it. "Help yourself," she said, grabbing a handful of chips.

I perched on the edge of the bed. The tray held chips and blueberries and gummy bears and two kinds of soda: root beer and Dr Pepper. She must be showing off—no way could all of this food be normal for an after-school snack. I wanted to grab fistfuls of everything, but I tried to act like it was no big deal as I scooped up a handful of chips and stuffed them into my mouth.

"Have a pop," she said.

I grabbed a Dr Pepper and cracked it open. Larry didn't think kids should drink caffeine or sugar, so I hadn't had one since forever.

Leigh tossed a few blueberries in her mouth and then somersaulted across her bed. She really was incapable of sitting still for more than two seconds at a time. I helped myself to the gummies and studied the rest of her room.

An antique lamp that had been bedazzled with crystals sat on a bedside table. Her dresser was a rainbow, with the drawers on the left painted red, orange, and yellow, and the drawers on the right painted green, blue, and the same purple as her headboard. A neat desk was tucked in the corner. A rainbow-colored flag stuck up out of an assortment of pens that must have come as a set rather than snatched from whatever business offered them for free.

I'd thought Leigh had been pulled toward Ava's orbit this morning the same way everyone else was, but now I wondered if it had something to do with the rainbows. Judging by the way Ava had been smiling at Tyler before school, I didn't think Leigh stood a chance, but it was none of my business.

As if she'd read my mind, Leigh asked, "So how well do you know Ava Benson?"

She was trying to keep her voice casual, but she was sitting up straight.

"She lives in one of the fancy houses over on the other side of town. Her dad is one of the bigwigs at the coal mine." I struggled with what to say next. "She's the most popular girl in our grade, but that might be more because people are afraid of her than because they like her."

"She can't be that bad," Leigh said.

Over the summer, I'd gone out to play on the tractor and found a rattler coiled on the seat, showing off its diamond pattern. As cool as it was, getting close would have meant a poisonous bite for sure. "She's like a rattlesnake," I said. "You're better off keeping your distance."

Leigh studied her nails. "She probably has something going on at home. My mom says it's important not to judge a book by its cover."

My mom always said that, too, but I thought it was a dumb saying. A cover could tell you what to expect from a book, and it was the same with Ava—I'd learned a long time ago that the fancier someone was on the outside, the meaner they were on the inside.

A tiny bit of doubt prickled inside me as I crunched on a chip and studied Leigh's fancy clothes. Maybe she was an exception to the rule. Still, I was certain that Ava didn't have anything bad going on at home. Both her parents drove expensive cars, and her mom used to be a fashion designer. Ava pretty much had a new wardrobe every week.

Leigh changed the subject. "I want to paint the ceiling black and put stars on it," she said. "But Mom says we have to wait until the rest of the trailer is unpacked."

I didn't know what to say. We'd moved into an apartment once that had gross pictures drawn all over the living room walls. We'd bought a gallon of paint to cover it up, and Mom had grumbled that we should have gotten a discount on our rent since the paint cost half a week's worth of groceries. I couldn't imagine asking her to paint my ceiling for fun.

"What's your room like?" Leigh asked.

"Oh, you know," I said vaguely. "Pretty boring." The last thing I was going to do was tell her about the moldy carpet smell or the sound of the mice running around in the walls.

"What's your color scheme?" she asked.

"My color scheme?"

"Yeah, like obviously mine is purple with rainbow accents. Every room should have a color scheme to tie it all together. I'm going to be an interior decorator when I grow up, so I know all about this stuff."

I couldn't believe she knew anything about interior

decorating—that was something I thought only *really* rich people could afford.

"Wait," Leigh said. "Let me guess. You don't seem like a gray or black kind of girl, but you definitely aren't pink either. Red, maybe? Or yellow? No, that's a little too sunny. Blue? I give up. What is it?"

If I had my choice, my entire room would be covered in my favorite color: teal. But in reality, the walls were a pukey beige-green color, and there wasn't anything in it except the yellow raft and an upside-down box I used as a nightstand. And now a bright pink elephant.

"Yellow, I guess?"

"Really?" Leigh said. "Huh. I wouldn't have taken you for the yellow type, but as Mom always says, we all contain multitudes."

I didn't think I contained a multitude of anything. And I had no idea what my type was, but I was pretty sure it couldn't be figured out by the color raft I slept in.

Leigh arched backwards off the bed, landed on her hands, pushed herself into a bridge, and then walked her feet overhead and ended up standing.

"Shouldn't we get started on the applications?" I asked.

"Good point," Leigh said.

I eyed the unfinished treats, wondering if we'd have to leave them behind when we went to use the computer.

Leigh laughed. "How about I type and you eat?"

I blushed, embarrassed that my longing had been so obvious.

She pulled a laptop out from her desk drawer, and I nearly fell off the bed.

"You have your own laptop?" Our laptops had been issued at school that morning, but we weren't allowed to bring them home.

She shrugged. "That way Mom and I don't fight when she needs to edit photos and I want to work on design stuff."

"I didn't know photographers made that much money."

"It's not like we're rich or anything. But Mom does a couple of shows in New York each year and has some work in galleries out on the West Coast, so she does okay."

Okay? Leigh had served more snacks in one afternoon than I got in a year. And she dressed like a fashion model, slept in a bed fit for a princess, and had her own computer. I'd say her mom did way more than okay. I tried to imagine Mom and I sharing this trailer—just the two of us, with no Larry in sight. Leigh had no idea how lucky she was.

"Besides, I'm not doing gymnastics anymore. That makes things easier."

Gymnastics explained how she was always bouncing around, and all of her muscles, but I wondered about the bitter note in her voice.

"Can't you do gymnastics here?"

Leigh shrugged.

She obviously didn't want to talk about it. There were plenty of things I didn't want to talk about, so I let the subject drop.

She settled back on a mountain of fluffy pillows and opened her laptop. "Let's start with your application."

I guzzled Dr Pepper and fought the urge to burp.

The application started with easy things like my address and birthday, but then it got more difficult. For one thing, I had to write a short essay telling them why I wanted to participate. I wasn't about to share the real reason with anyone.

Leigh came to my rescue and helped me write a paragraph about how enriching the opportunity would be. She added a bunch more stuff about the honor of representing the coal mine in the community and saving the winnings for college, but I was stuck on the enrichment part—she meant for my mind, but the only thing I was interested in enriching was my pockets.

"What's your talent?" Leigh asked, interrupting my thoughts.

I nearly spit out my Dr Pepper. "My talent?"

"You know, what you're going to show the judges?"

"Oh, um . . ." My mind was totally blank. I didn't have any talents that I knew of.

"Have you ever taken dance?"

I shook my head.

"Can you draw?"

"Last year I tried to draw a gray wolf in art class. My teacher thought it was a goat."

"Okay, so no drawing. What about music—do you play any instruments?"

I was starting to really hate this pageant.

"What about singing?"

I straightened. "Yeah, I can sing."

I hadn't taken lessons or anything like that, but I loved singing along to the music on Mom's phone before it broke, and sometimes I even sang in the shower.

After that, Leigh asked for my height and weight and all my measurements. Since I had no idea, she borrowed her mom's scale and a measuring tape.

"This is stupid," I said while she was looking up how to measure my bust. "Why do they need our measurements?"

She shrugged. "To make sure we're pageant queen material, I guess."

I crossed my arms. That was code for making sure the contestants were all skinny. As if that's what made someone beautiful.

"Come on," Leigh said. "Uncross your arms so I can get this right."

I huffed but let her take my measurements. *Eyes on the prize*, I reminded myself.

"You've got a great figure," Leigh said. "You should show it off more."

Attracting attention, especially to my chest, was the last thing I wanted to do. Anyway, I couldn't exactly run out and get a whole new wardrobe.

"Okay," Leigh said after she'd crawled back on the bed and finished entering my numbers, "we just need to attach your photos and submit the registration fee."

I scowled. "A photo?"

"It says we need a headshot and at least one full body. Do you have any you can send me?"

I panicked. "I don't have a phone and my mom's is broke, remember? Can we take one on your phone?"

"We *could*," Leigh said. "But I really think we need to put our best foot forward from the very beginning."

She set the laptop on her nightstand, sprang to her feet, and started jumping on the bed. I bobbed up and down, trying to keep my balance.

"Let's have a photo shoot," she said. "We can do our hair and makeup and Mom can take our pictures. It'll be so much fun!"

It didn't sound fun. Mom used to make me sit still for what felt like hours as she tried to comb the tangles from my hair. Between that and makeup, Leigh's idea sounded like torture. Medieval torture, like when they used to hang people by their thumbs. I scrambled for an excuse. "That'll take too long. Let's snap a picture with your mom's phone and get it over with."

Leigh put her hands on her hips. "Fud," she said, "This pageant is no joke. Hundreds of girls are sure to enter, and they only accept thirty contestants."

Only thirty? I was no math wiz, but the odds were definitely not in my favor.

"You don't think Ava is going to send in photos she snapped at the very last minute, do you?"

She got me there. As much as I didn't want to do a photo shoot, I also didn't want to take any chances on Ava Benson winning before the pageant had even started.

"Fine." My stomach felt a little shaky, but I couldn't tell if it was from all the treats or the idea of doing a photo shoot.

"Let me see when Mom can do it."

While she was gone, I eyed the last few gummy bears. Maybe I'd get lucky and they would come to life and gobble me up so that I didn't have to go through with this.

Leigh bounded back through the door. "She's free Saturday!"

Half-digested Dr Pepper bubbled from my guts, filling my throat. I managed a weak smile as I jumped to my feet and explained that I had to get home. I blamed it on home-work and chores, but the truth was that if I stuck around this place much longer, I'd end up spewing regurgitated gummy bears across Leigh's perfectly decorated bedroom.

CHAPTER SIX

The next morning, Mom reclined on the couch holding an ice cube folded in a washcloth over her eye.

"Morning," she said.

"Morning," I mumbled.

"You okay?" She dropped the bundle and sat up. The swelling around her eye had gone down, but the bruising was worse. My fist clenched. I wished I could give Larry a big old shiner in return.

"Tired. Stupid coyotes hardly let me sleep." Even if a nearby pack hadn't kept me up, I would have been awake anyway, listening for sounds that Larry was beating up Mom again.

"Coyotes?" Mom cocked her head.

"The ones that held the sing-along all night?"

"That's strange," she said, rubbing her forehead. "I didn't hear a thing."

"You're joking, right?" Mom was the world's lightest sleeper. She always claimed that she could hear it if I so much as rolled over at night.

"It must have been a dream," she said.

It was definitely not, but I ignored the squirming in my gut and let the subject go. I had to get moving if I wanted to catch the bus.

"What's for breakfast?" I asked, scanning the stove for the usual pot of oatmeal.

"Make yourself two sandwiches and eat one now."

Her eye must be worse than I thought—she'd never missed making me breakfast before. I was plenty old enough to do it myself, but that didn't stop another wave of anger from hitting me. I shouldn't *have* to do it myself.

I spread crunchy peanut butter across two slices of bread, wrinkling my nose as I added just enough peach jelly so I could swallow the peanut butter.

I said goodbye to Mom and stomped out of the trailer, wishing there was some way to get to the bus without walking past Leigh's and subjecting myself to her good mood. A door slammed after I passed her trailer. I groaned.

"Fud," she called.

I kept walking.

"Hey, what's with the boat in your driveway?" she asked, catching up.

My throat squeezed shut. Telling her Larry's plan might make it real. "Just another one of Larry's projects."

"That's cool," she said, tucking her white shirt into breezy linen pants. "But where's he going to use it?"

The words squirmed around in my mouth like worms stuck on a fishing hook, so I shrugged.

Luckily, Leigh moved on. "I can't wait for our photo shoot. I've already picked out what I'm going to wear. What about you?"

"Hadn't really thought about it." I wished I could crawl back in my raft and cover my head with a pillow. I hadn't gotten enough sleep to deal with pageant talk this morning.

She didn't take the hint. "If you want, I can come over tonight and help you pick something out. It's important not to wear patterns or black and white. And an interesting neckline is always good for headshots."

I swallowed, my throat suddenly dry. I didn't exactly have a whole lot to choose from—if Mom made it to the Laundromat, I might have a clean T-shirt. But as I opened my mouth to tell Leigh that I'd changed my mind, Mom's shiner popped into my head. I had to get her—get both of us—out of this place.

"I'm good." I'd do the dumb shoot, but no way was I inviting Leigh over to rummage through my nonexistent wardrobe.

"Okay," she said. "If you change your mind, you know where to find me."

She continued on, showing me her bright blue nails and chattering about whether to change the color before the shoot. I yawned, then cursed the coyotes again for keeping me up.

As soon as I reached homeroom, I logged onto my laptop. Most of the websites about coyotes covered stuff I already knew, like their diets (they're omnivores and eat practically anything), their eyesight (they're color-blind except for blues and yellows but have excellent peripheral vision), and their gestation period (they're pregnant for 63 days). But I finally found a website that talked about coyote communication and shared some recordings.

Scientists had identified about a dozen different coyote vocalizations and had a general idea of how they were used, but I was surprised to find that no one really understood the nuances of how they communicated. Part of that was because they were experts at tricking people. Two coyotes could make themselves sound like seven or eight!

I listened to the recordings while I skimmed the descriptions, committing as much of it as I could to memory.

That night, I perked up when the coyotes started with their racket. I'd figured their howls and barking the night before had something to do with a particularly speedy jackrabbit. Or a deer or a gopher or some other animal they were determined to eat. In reality, they were probably either marking their location or signaling their territory. They filled the air with the barks, howls, yips, and yowls that had always set me on edge. Tonight, the sounds wrapped around me snug as a warm blanket in the dead of winter, and I fell asleep wishing I could understand.

The rest of the week, I listened carefully, trying to make any kind of sense out of the coyote's calls. I couldn't identify individual voices, much less understand their conversations, but with each passing night, I felt more connected to them, more like we were all tied together with an invisible string. It tugged at me like a knot I couldn't quite undo.

Saturday morning, I pulled on my cleanest T-shirt and jeans before sliding into my shoes at the trailer's door.

"Where you going?" Larry asked from his chair. He had a can of Bud Light in one hand and a boxing magazine in the other. He'd stormed around all morning complaining that he couldn't work on the boat because of the gosh darn rain (only he didn't use those words) and mumbling about what in the heck he was supposed to do all day. Mom had stayed in bed because she wasn't feeling great again. I'd thought she was acting differently on account of her black eye, but maybe she was coming down with something.

"Leigh's."

"What for?"

"A photo shoot." Although I was dreading the ordeal, there was a small part of me that was glad to have an excuse to leave the trailer.

"What kind of photo shoot?"

"Just for fun. Leigh's mom is a photographer." I wasn't sure why I didn't tell him about the pageant. I was worried he'd say I couldn't do it, I guessed. Or worse, that he'd figure out *why* I was doing it.

"What's that going to cost me?" He settled farther into his chair and put up his feet on the coffee table.

"Nothing," I said. "It's free."

He didn't seem to have anything to say to that, so I pulled open the door, eager to escape.

"No makeup," he said as I stepped outside.

I did my best not to slam the door behind me. I wasn't really interested in makeup, but earlier in the summer I'd asked Mom for some of the tinted lip gloss that all the girls at school were wearing. Somehow, she came up with the money for a tube, but Larry made me throw it away because he said I didn't need to make myself look any older than I was.

It was pouring rain, but I wasn't about to go back for an umbrella.

I stormed through the yard, ignoring the mud that splattered around me. Larry wasn't my dad—his nose didn't belong in my business. As I climbed the stairs to Leigh's trailer, my face burned with anger.

She pulled open the door and laughed. "You're soaked!"

I stepped inside. Her mom was clearing a plate of

delicious-smelling pancakes and pineapple from the table. "You poor thing. Let me get you a towel."

She disappeared into the back hall.

I stood dripping in the doorway. Only a giant idiot would show up for a photo shoot soaking wet. Instead of cooling down, the burning on my face turned into an angry itch. It was like there were red stinging ants running around under my skin, starting under my cheeks and scurrying up to my forehead. I reached up to scratch, wondering if I was having some kind of allergic reaction. But to what? My lips twisted into a smirk. I was probably allergic to Larry.

I kicked off my shoes and forced myself to stop rubbing at my face. Click and Leigh seemed to be almost completely moved in. Most of the boxes were gone. An emerald-colored velvet couch rested up against the wall, and a coffee table that looked as if it had started out as a suitcase squatted in front of it. Another of their upcycling projects, probably.

The rest of the room was filled with plants and lamps and a life-sized statue of a peacock. Absolutely nothing matched and yet somehow everything was perfect.

Click rushed back into the room and wrapped me in the biggest, fluffiest towel I'd ever seen. Ours were all small pieces, worn through and scratchy. This was practically a blanket—a soft, fuzzy blanket. I dried off my still-itching face and followed Click's orders to throw the damp towel over a chair at the table.

"I was hoping we could do the shoot outside," Click said. "But we'll have to do our best with the lighting in here."

She motioned toward the corner, where bright lights shone down on a stool with a screen behind it. Hopefully, this would go quickly. I didn't want to be in the spotlight any longer than I had to be.

Leigh looked me up and down. "Did you bring something to change into?"

She was wearing brand-new jeans and a thin, green V-neck sweater. Heat nipped at my cheeks. It wasn't as if I had anything that nice.

She grabbed me by the hand and pulled me toward her bedroom. "Come on," she said cheerfully. "I'm sure I have something. But let's do our hair and makeup first."

The bathroom, which smelled like the cosmetics section of a drugstore, wasn't really big enough for both of us to stand in front of the mirror, so I hovered in the doorway while Leigh brushed her long, golden hair. "I can't decide whether to wear it straight or do some curls. What do you think?"

"Curls," I said, trying to sound like I knew what I was talking about.

"You think?" She reached over and plugged in something that looked like a flat curling iron.

I continued standing in the doorway, feeling more out

of place by the second as she pulled open a drawer cluttered with makeup.

"Mom says I have to be thirteen to wear makeup out of the house, but she lets me wear concealer and lip gloss whenever I want. I bet she won't mind a little mascara today, either." She opened a tube of concealer and dotted some skin-colored cream under her eyes.

"Here," she said, handing me the tube.

I hesitated. Larry would kill me if he found out.

"You want me to do it?" Leigh turned away from the mirror.

I knew I should say no, but my head nodded yes. My face had stopped itching, but I probably needed concealer after the scratching I'd done. Leigh dotted the tip of her finger with some of the cream. "Your skin is darker than mine," she said. "But this will do in a pinch."

I stood still as she patted it under my eyes, breathing gently on me with her pineapple-scented breath. Every once in a while, Mom brought home a can of pineapple as a special treat. It always came out in small, wet pieces— nothing even close to the big chunks of fresh pineapple I'd spotted on the table.

Leigh stood back to admire her work. "Maybe a touch of mascara, too. You have amazing lashes."

"No mascara." I pulled my head back. Larry wouldn't notice a little concealer, but mascara was a whole different story.

"Come on," Leigh said. "It'll really define your eyes."

"I'm not allowed."

"You're going to have to wear makeup for the pageant, so you might as well practice now. We can wash it off before you go home."

Despite the warning bells clanging in my belly, I gave in and followed her directions, rolling my eyeballs up to the ceiling while she feathered the mascara on my lashes. When she finished, she pulled back to inspect her work. She nodded, satisfied, then scanned the rest of my face.

"You have great eyebrows, too."

The announcement surprised me. I'd never thought about my eyebrows one way or another.

"They could use a little shaping, but I don't want to do that right before pictures," she said.

I peered in the mirror. She was obviously trying not to embarrass me. How was it possible that I never noticed how bushy my eyebrows were? The burning returned to my face. "Don't you think we should fix them now?"

"We don't want your skin to be pink in the photos. You're so gorgeous it won't matter anyway."

Now that she'd pointed out my eyebrows, I couldn't stop staring. I tried to smooth the thick patches of hair into some kind of order, but they still looked wrong. I had the strange feeling I sometimes got when I spelled out a word correctly but then it didn't look like a real word at all—these were obviously my eyebrows, but they didn't feel like my eyebrows. They felt alien, like someone's mustache had been transplanted onto my face.

I pulled myself away from the mirror and waited on Leigh's bed while she worked on her hair.

Her closet doors were open, revealing so many clothes that she could practically have her own department store. They were arranged in rainbow-color order. A jean jacket tucked in with the blues jumped out at me. I glanced down at my grubby T-shirt and swallowed. Mom had a strict rule about never asking for anything—she said no good could come of owing something you might not be able to pay back. But this was different—Leigh had already offered to lend me clothes.

I was saved from making the decision when she walked out of the bathroom and saw what I was staring at. "You should totally borrow that! It'll look great on you!"

She pulled the coat from the closet. I slipped my arms in. The jacket was too tight to close around my chest, but it fit otherwise.

"Perfect!" Leigh said.

The only thing perfect were the curls hanging around her face.

She patted one into place. "What do you think?"

"You look terrific," I said honestly.

"Thank God for flat irons."

Flat iron. I tucked the term away in my vocabulary and wondered how she knew all this stuff. It was like she'd been born with fashion sense, like it was in her DNA. My DNA didn't have anything in it about how to look good. For a long time, my DNA was too worried about where we were going to live and where our next meal would come from.

Leigh helped coax my still-damp curls into a ponytail. "Just a bit of lip gloss and you'll be all set."

The sticky gloss made my lips feel like they were covered in honey, but when I studied myself in the mirror, I was glad I'd tried it.

The changes were subtle, but somehow, a different person looked back at me—someone who would never be stuck sleeping on a raft. I saw now what Click meant about my cheekbones, how they were high and hollow underneath. I looked like the girls I saw in the magazines on the grocery store stands.

A bubble of hope expanded in my chest. Maybe I really did have a shot at getting in the pageant.

When we entered the living room, Click smiled. "You two are going to make my job easy," she said. "Who's up first?"

"You want to go?" Leigh asked.

"Nah, you go ahead."

She skipped over to the stool and plunked down. She'd obviously done this a million times before. Click fiddled with the lighting and then started snapping photos, filling the air with harsh clicks. Her camera had a long lens that made it look old-fashioned, but the screen on the back told me it was digital. At first, I paid close attention to Leigh so I'd know what to do, but then I started looking around.

A strange collection of photos hung on the wall over the couch. Most of them I recognized as younger versions of Leigh, but they weren't the happy, sparkly Leigh I knew. They were black-and-white, and heavily shadowed, and if I was being honest, super creepy. In one, Leigh sank back in an armchair but her eyes were blurred out. In another, the wind tousled her hair. A pair of man's hands gripped her arms as she glowered at the camera. In the most shocking photo, she was much younger and wearing a frilly white dress but holding a lit cigarette. A cigarette!

"What do you think of my work?" Click called.

I hadn't realized she'd been watching me. I couldn't exactly tell her the truth about how weird her photos were.

"Um," I said.

"It's okay. You can be honest."

I didn't want to say anything that might make her mad. "It's . . . interesting."

She laughed. "Good. Art should be interesting. I like giving people the unexpected. Making them think."

Creeping them out, I thought, but I didn't say it out loud. "So, our photos . . ."

She laughed again. "You don't have to worry. I'll leave my artistic inclinations out of it."

I hoped that meant we'd get normal photos. I couldn't imagine applying with anything close to what she had hanging on the wall.

"We're finished over here," she said. "Your turn."

Chatting with Click had helped me relax a little, but taking the spotlight made my stomach jump like it was filled with frogs.

"Don't be nervous," Leigh said.

That's what doctors always said before they gave shots. And teachers before they gave tests. The frogs leaped even higher. While Click double-checked the lighting, I hovered near the stool, reminding myself that I was doing all this for a reason.

"I think we're about ready." Click approached me, holding her camera in one hand. She used the other to smooth back my curls and adjust my ponytail over my shoulder. After that, she arranged me on the stool in a way that I was certain would look awful in the photos.

"Should I smile?"

"Only if you feel like it."

I felt like vomiting.

"Okay, well, maybe try not to look like you're Little Red Riding Hood and I'm the Big Bad Wolf."

I couldn't help it. My lips turned up a little.

"Perfect," she said. "Hold it there."

Holding a smile wasn't as easy as it sounded.

"Go to your happy place," she called out.

My happy place? Until recently, that would have been anywhere Mom was. But these days, anywhere Mom was usually meant Larry was close by. The smile fell off my face.

"Come on," Click said, "you must have something worth smiling about."

Easy for her to say. She probably never worried about a single thing in her entire life. I imagined being her kid. Sleeping in Leigh's bed. Having an unlimited supply of food and clothes. Actually *wanting* to do a beauty pageant. For fun, not because winning might be the only way to save my mom's life.

The bright light Click had aimed at me burned into my skin, searing it with the heat of a thousand suns.

Click went her camera.

An image of being trapped on the boat with Larry popped into my head. He was drinking, and there was nowhere to run.

Click.

The light burned brighter, like it wasn't trying to highlight my face so much as give her a way to see all the way inside me.

Click.

The camera was impossibly loud. Everything was too loud. The hum of the fridge. Plastic rustling as Leigh opened a bag of chips. My own heart beating in my ears. A pool of tears welled behind my eyes. I tried to blink them back, but Click lowered her camera. Worried wrinkles appeared in her forehead. I could tell she was about to ask what was wrong. There was no way I could explain it to her. No way she'd understand.

The dam of tears broke. I jumped off the stool and bolted toward the door.

"Fud," Leigh yelled. "What's wrong? Come back!"

The door slammed behind me. I didn't slow down, not even when I realized I was still wearing Leigh's jacket.

CHAPTER SEVEN

It was still pouring outside, so I was drenched within seconds. As I entered the trailer, the wind grabbed the door and slammed it into the wall. Larry, who had apparently fallen asleep with a beer in his hand, woke up and let out a stream of obscenities ending with "What happened to you?"

"Nothing," I mumbled. "Got caught in the rain."

I wouldn't have minded a hug from Mom, but she was nowhere to be seen. Since I didn't exactly want to spend the rest of the afternoon with Larry, I headed straight for my room.

"Get back here," he called.

I closed my eyes and took a deep breath. Maybe he wanted something simple, like another beer.

"Yeah?" I asked once I stood in front of him.

"What's that on your face?"

Oh, no.

I swiped my cheek. Black mascara smudged my hand. "Um—"

Larry jumped up. His face flushed red. "I hope you have something better to say than 'um.'"

"I meant to wash it off," I said meekly. "It was for the pictures."

Larry slammed his Bud Light down on the coffee table. Golden liquid sloshed from the can.

"You meant to hide it from me, you mean."

"No," I protested. "It was only for pictures. I wasn't going to wear it around or anything."

"I said no makeup." Larry gripped my arm as he dragged me across the kitchen and down the hallway. "If I meant no makeup except for pictures, I would have said it. It's about time you learn how to listen."

His fingers dug into my skin. I squirmed, but he only squeezed tighter. Halfway down the hall, he stopped. Hope blossomed in my chest. Maybe he was letting me off with a warning to stay in my room for the day.

"Get in there." He shoved me into the bathroom.

A bison-sized rush of fear crushed my hope. Smells assaulted my already overwhelmed senses. Larry's aftershave. Shampoo. The Ajax we used to clean the toilet. I raced to the sink and began splashing ice-cold water on my face.

My head was jerked back, then slammed down into the stream coming from the faucet. I let out a surprised shriek as Larry gripped my hair with one hand and aggressively scrubbed my face with his other. When he was satisfied, he yanked me up and grabbed my tooth-brush from the counter.

I held back a strangled sob.

"It's about time you learn who's boss around here." He shoved my toothbrush in my hand.

My head burned from where he'd pulled my hair, and water dripped down the front of my body, and what did brushing my teeth have to do with him being boss?

"Start with the sink. When you're done with that, do the shower. And then the toilet. I'd better not find a single spot of dirt when you're done."

My brain couldn't keep up.

He squeezed my hand holding the toothbrush and brought it down to scrub around the faucet. I fought a nearly overwhelming urge to lean over and sink my teeth into the leathery flesh of his muscular hand.

"You don't stop until it's done, you hear me?"

He wanted me to scrub the bathroom with my *tooth-brush*? I focused on clenching my teeth together, afraid if I relaxed my jaw even a little, I'd snap.

The green handle of the toothbrush had a picture of Yoda on it. I'd been on a serious Star Wars kick last winter and had begged Mom for a battery-powered light saber toothbrush when I saw it at the grocery store. She said it wasn't in our budget, but when I woke up on Christmas morning, this one was tucked into my stocking alongside an orange and a pack of pencils.

After this, I'd have to throw the toothbrush out.

Larry stormed out of the room. I scrubbed furiously around the faucet as hot tears dripped into the sink and slid down the drain. I considered calling for Mom, but she'd probably take Larry's side, and I couldn't bear to hear that I'd asked for this.

My hand ached from squeezing the toothbrush, but I kept working. I'd finished the sink and shower and moved on to scrubbing the pegs on the toilet when Mom walked in wearing a pair of old sweats. Her hair was limp and stringy like she hadn't brushed it for a few days.

She saw me kneeling on the floor and wrinkled her nose. "What in the world are you doing?"

"Cleaning the bathroom."

"With your *toothbrush*?"

"It wasn't exactly my choice."

"There must have been a misunderstanding," she said. "Larry would never ask you to do that."

He didn't exactly ask. I kept scrubbing.

"Put that toothbrush down," Mom said, backing up. "I'll talk to him and sort things out."

"No," I said, lunging for her. "It's no big deal!"

She stared at me like I'd lost my mind. Maybe I had. Or maybe I couldn't bear the thought of Mom walking around with *two* black eyes.

* * *

Sunshine flooded my room. As I stretched, a nightmare replayed itself in my mind. I'd been a coyote, but instead of playing with a pack of pups, I'd spent the night gnawing on a bone I somehow knew had once been Larry's leg. My stanky morning breath suddenly tasted metallic. I ran to the bathroom, freezing when I noticed my missing toothbrush.

Fury reignited inside my chest. Mom always said anger was a fire that started small but burned brighter with oxygen. I wanted to let my hatred go, but I couldn't—not as long as Larry was in charge.

With jerky movements, I rolled up the nearly empty toothpaste and forced what was left to snake its way onto my pointer finger, a trick Mom taught me when we were living out of The Miracle. I reached into my mouth. A sharp tooth pressed into the soft flesh on the tip of my finger. *That's strange.* I pulled my hand from my mouth and peered in the mirror. Two vampire fangs stuck out where my regular teeth normally were. I shut my eyes.

This can't be happening. Vampires aren't real.

I ran my tongue over my teeth. They didn't feel like fangs. I opened my eyes and inspected my teeth in the mirror. My smile was completely normal.

I rinsed the gritty, baking-soda-flavored paste from my mouth and filled my chest with deep, calming breaths. Mom always said I had a wild imagination.

I shook my head as I turned off the faucet. Larry must really be getting to me.

He was lucky I wasn't a vampire—I'd never let him get away with any of this.

Larry was nowhere in sight when I entered the kitchen, but Mom was scrambling eggs, which surprised me because I didn't know we had any, and she hadn't been getting out of bed in time for breakfast lately.

A bouquet of flowers sat in the middle of the table. They were real, but the colors were so bright they seemed fake. A plain pink toothbrush rested in a package beside them.

"Larry brought me flowers," Mom said brightly. "And he replaced your toothbrush."

I wanted to smash the gifts up against the wall. It was like we were already on Larry's boat, only instead of smooth sailing, a storm tossed us side to side so we couldn't catch our balance. "Is he trying to bribe us?"

"Of course not!" Mom glanced up sharply. "He's apologizing."

I crossed my arms and glared at the stupid pink toothbrush. "Apology not accepted."

She wiped her hands on a kitchen towel. "We have to cut him some slack. He's exhausted working full time and trying to get the boat ready."

"I'll cut him some slack when he stops treating us like a pile of dried-up cow chips."

"Listen," Mom said. "He snapped. But he apologized, and he said it would never happen again. We need to put this behind us."

I couldn't believe she was making excuses for him. And I especially couldn't believe she really thought he'd never do anything like this again because he bought her some stinking flowers. "Where is he?"

"Outside. He's sealing the boat today so he can get the painting done next weekend."

While I was at school last week, one of his buddies from the mine brought out a small crane and a bunch of lumber. They'd built a sort of scaffold for the boat so he could do the repairs.

She set a plate of fluffy eggs in front of me. I poured salt over them and shoveled a bite into my mouth.

Mom scrubbed a frying pan at the sink. "What's on your agenda today?"

Usually, I loved how grown-up this question made me feel.

A blush built as I thought about apologizing to Leigh and her mother for how I'd acted, but there was no way around it—I couldn't give up on the pageant, and I couldn't do it without them. Besides, I'd kind of gotten used to Leigh. I didn't want to go back to the way things were before she showed up.

"Nothing much. I'll probably mess around outside."

"Larry could use a hand," she said, drying the pan.

I jumped up to wash my plate with a dingy sponge and the dishwater Mom had left in a small bowl at the bottom of the sink. No way was I going to help speed up our one-way ticket to doom.

"What does Larry know about driving a boat? What if we end up shipwrecked somewhere and they never find us?"

Mom settled onto the couch. "You mean helming a boat?"

"Whatever."

"He's smart, and he has all winter to figure it out. Anyway, it's not like we'll ever be far from civilization."

I was happy he wasn't planning to drag us out of here anytime soon. But still. "The middle of the ocean is pretty far from civilization."

"The ocean?" Mom laughed as she picked up a half-finished book. "Where in the world did you get that idea?"

"Where else will we sail the boat?"

"Larry's dream has always been to sail up and down the Mississippi."

I'd thought his dream was to be a boxing champion. But I was glad there was no chance we'd end up in the middle of the ocean with no land in sight. On the other hand—the Mississippi?

Mom couldn't really think this was a good idea.

Not that it mattered. We weren't getting on that boat with him no matter where he was planning to sail it. I reached in my pocket to make sure the twenty I'd grabbed after getting dressed was there. With a little luck, my five-dollar registration would be our ticket out of this place.

I didn't see Larry, but the smell of whatever chemical he was using to seal a crack in the hull followed me all the way to Leigh's, giving me the courage to raise my fist and knock on the door. Leigh answered holding a piece of bacon. She was still in pajamas, but she didn't seem to care.

"Fud!" she squealed, practically yanking me inside. "I was worried about you yesterday, but Mom said everybody has off days, and the lights can be overwhelming, and I should just give you some space. Still, I was worried you'd changed your mind or you wouldn't come back. Sit down. We're just finishing breakfast. Let me get the pictures. You won't believe how good they are!"

I'd grabbed Leigh's jean jacket before leaving Larry's trailer. I folded it over the back of a chair and sat down.

Click had already pulled an extra plate from the cupboard. "The pancakes are leftover from yesterday," she apologized. "But the bacon is fresh, and I cut up some mango. Help yourself."

As she talked, she heaped food on my plate. I thought about telling her I'd already eaten, but one egg had barely put a dent in my hunger, and even the bacon, which I usually couldn't stand, was making my mouth water.

"Do you eat like this every day?" Mom only made

bacon once a month, and that was only because Larry insisted she find room in the budget.

Click laughed. "On weekends. During the week, it's mostly cold cereal or smoothies. Here," she said, handing me a jug of syrup. "Don't be stingy."

I doused my pancakes, feeling like I'd won the lottery. I'd come over expecting to grovel. Instead, I was being given the royal treatment.

That didn't mean how I'd acted had been okay.

"I'm sorry for running out of here yesterday," I said as Leigh returned with her laptop.

"No apology necessary," Click said.

"The important thing is that you're here now," Leigh added, sliding her computer toward me. "The pictures are perfect!"

I couldn't believe that was really true. But when I started clicking through photos, I had to admit I was impressed. Leigh's pictures were great, of course, but even mine were decent. Click must have snapped the headshot right as she made the joke about Little Red Riding Hood because there was a gleam of laughter that I wasn't used to seeing in my eyes. She'd also taken a few full-body shots before we'd officially started. My bare feet seemed on purpose and the jacket dressed up my scruffy jeans. Even my eyebrows somehow looked good. If I didn't know better, I'd think I was a normal girl without a care in the world.

"Should we finish our applications?" I asked.

Leigh reclaimed the computer and moved her finger around the touchpad. "I already attached the photos. All we need to do is hit submit."

I stared at her, dumbstruck. I'd run out on her, and she'd still done all this work for me.

"Thanks."

She grinned. "No biggie."

I didn't know what to say, so I asked the other question on my mind. "What about our application fee?"

"I used Mom's credit card. You can pay her back whenever."

I pulled the twenty out of my pocket and slid it across the table.

"Let me find my purse," Click said, rising from her chair. "I can probably make change."

"You ready to hit submit?" Leigh asked.

I pulled in a deep breath. Applying was no guarantee I'd get in, but it still felt big. Like the first step in getting out of here. I imagined the apartment Mom and I would get with the money. I didn't care if it had one bedroom or two or if I still had to sleep in my raft. Heck, I didn't care if we got an apartment at all—I'd gladly sleep in whatever car Mom bought if it meant we were free of Larry. But first, I had to win, and to do that, I had to apply. "Do it."

Leigh tapped the touchpad.

"That's it," she said. "We're entered."

I lifted my eyebrows. "We're *both* entered?"

"I did my application earlier."

I flushed, embarrassed all over again that I'd left her to do everything herself. "I should probably get going."

"Don't go," she said, pouting. "You just got here."

She brightened and clapped her hands, something I'd realized she did whenever she had an idea I wasn't going to like. "I talked Mom into taking me to the mall to start shopping for a dress. Come with us." She clasped her hands together like she was praying. "Please!"

Trying on dresses I could never afford to buy for a pageant I hadn't gotten into yet didn't exactly sound fun, but I had to admit going to the mall with Leigh would be better than sitting around Larry's trailer. "Let me ask."

I didn't think Mom would care, but she hemmed and hawed. "I don't know," she said, layering a coat of red polish over the nail on her ring finger. "You're awfully young to be hanging out at the mall."

I had the urge to sink my teeth into her bony wrist. Not to hurt her, but to make her listen. "Mom, I'm in *seventh* grade! And we won't be there alone—Leigh's mom will be with us."

That finally won her over. "Fine," she said. "But take a granola bar for lunch. Those food courts charge an arm and a leg."

I was so glad she'd said yes that I didn't bother

arguing. A minute later, I was back at Leigh's house, pulling stuffed animals from a box while we waited for her mom.

"I had a bookcase in my old room," Leigh said. "Here I really only have my bed and the top of my dresser, so I'm thinking maybe we should ignore what kind of animals they are and arrange them by color across my dresser, like a rainbow."

I liked that idea.

As we worked, I thought about Leigh's old room. It hadn't really occurred to me that she'd moved *from* somewhere. "Do you miss it?"

"Cheyenne?"

"No, the moon," I said, grinning and throwing a stuffed moose at her. It bounced off her shoulder and fell on the floor. "Of course Cheyenne."

"Not really." She picked up the moose. "Mom says there's no sense dwelling in the past when there's an entire future waiting to be explored."

Her words were upbeat, but she didn't sound like she really believed them. I decided to change the subject. There was a photo frame on her dresser, but it was turned around to face the wall. I reached for it, thinking it might be from the shoot yesterday.

A family grinned up at me. The old guy was pretty handsome for someone with graying hair. He gazed adoringly at the gorgeous woman standing next to him cradling a plump infant in her arms. "What a cute baby!"

Leigh set the moose on the dresser and headed for the bathroom.

When I was younger, I'd always hoped Mom would have another kid so I'd have someone to play with. Now, I'd never wish a life with Larry on a baby. "Who are they?"

"That's my dad and his new family." She glowered at the bathroom mirror as though she hated her reflection.

I'd assumed her dad was out of the picture. "You're so lucky to have a little sister!"

"Half sister," Leigh said quickly.

I didn't see why that mattered. A sister was a sister.

She continued frowning as she collected her hair at the back of her head. "Do you think I should wear my hair in a ponytail?"

I set down the photo and shrugged. "You look great both ways."

"Do you think so?"

"I wouldn't have said it if I didn't."

The sparkle returned to Leigh's eyes, and her whole face brightened. She crossed the room and gripped me in a hug. "I knew we were going to be best friends."

I didn't hug her back, but I didn't try to wriggle away, either.

CHAPTER EIGHT

The passenger's window crank in The Miracle had been broken when we bought it, so the window could only be rolled up or down with a pair of pliers we kept in the cubby. Click's car not only had windows that rolled up and down with the push of a button, but it also had a working radio, air-conditioning, and leather seats.

I buckled myself in on the passenger's side of the backseat. Leigh sat behind her mom. A new-car smell mixed with the strawberry scent of Leigh's shampoo. Click pushed a button, and the car hummed.

"You don't need a key?" I asked.

Click laughed. "I have a key in my purse. As long as it's nearby, the car will start."

Riding in a car without a key made me feel like anything was possible. I looked down, half-expecting to see my fingers dripping in diamonds. Not that I wanted to drip with diamonds, exactly. It was just, well . . . I adjusted my seatbelt, which had creeped up so that it was closer to my neck than stretched across my chest. This was all normal for Leigh—riding in a fancy car, shopping at the mall. I hadn't been to the mall since I'd outgrown the free toddler play areas where Mom used to take me to "run out my wilds" on cold winter days.

Whenever we needed something we couldn't find at a yard sale, we always ended up at one of the big box stores around town. Mom hated them on account of how they robbed their workers by not paying living wages, but she couldn't fight the fact that they had the lowest prices around.

Click steered down our gravel road in a sleeveless shirt. Her tattoo winked at me from her upper arm.

"Why do you have a fish tattoo?" I asked, only thinking better of it when the words were already out. I braced for her to say that it was none of my gosh darn business and to keep my mouth shut.

She turned the car onto the highway and then rubbed her arm. "It's to remind me to get out and live my life."

I wasn't sure how a goldfish could do that.

"Mom was sick when she was little," Leigh said.

"Real sick," Click said. "Leukemia. Spent years in and out of hospitals, and even when I wasn't sick, I was weak. My parents were overprotective and wouldn't let me do anything. I sat at home and stared out the windows as the world passed me by. I vowed that when

I recovered, I'd get out and live my life. When I get scared, I have this guy to remind me of what it felt like to be stuck inside."

"What do you have to be scared of now?"

Click laughed. "You'd be surprised."

I hoped she'd say more, but "Girls Just Want to Have Fun" came on the radio.

"I love this song!" She cranked up the music. It was one of my favorites, too. Before we moved in with Larry, Mom and I used to play it when we cleaned whatever apartment we were living in at the time. We'd turn it up full volume and dance around with a broom, pretending it was a microphone. Larry couldn't handle loud music—it gave him a headache because of all the concussions he'd suffered in the ring.

Click started singing. Her voice was so good she belonged on the radio. Leigh elbowed me, and we both joined in. Leigh didn't seem to care that she was slightly off-key. When the song ended, we belted out the next one and kept it up all the way to the mall.

Delicious smells called to me from the food court as Leigh and I followed Click to a store called Glitz and Glamour. Creepy headless mannequins wearing sequined gowns stood in the window.

I was tempted to tuck my tail and run the second we stepped foot inside. The store was filled with fancy dresses and sparkling jewelry fit for a queen. The place even smelled like money—like regular air wasn't good enough to breathe and had to be scented with flowery perfume.

A sales clerk with ghostly white skin, too much blush, and a bright red smile greeted us. She was dressed in a pantsuit with a lace shirt underneath. Her spiked heels were about ten feet high, and her golden hair was streaked with red highlights. A different flowery perfume wafted around her.

"These girls would like to try on dresses," Click announced, apparently not one bit bothered by the fact that she was wearing a sleeveless T-shirt and jeans.

I waited for the sales clerk to whisper, "Fuddy-dud," under her breath, which of course didn't make sense because she didn't know my name.

Instead of scanning my outfit and then wrinkling her nose or lifting an eyebrow, she smiled and asked, "You girls must be doing the pageant?"

"Yes!" Leigh said.

The sales clerk nodded. "Congratulations. I'm sure we'll find each of you the perfect dress."

My perfect dress would be one marked "free."

As we dug through the racks, I glanced at the price tags. My brain almost exploded. Some of these dresses were more than Mom used to pay for our rent. I shouldn't have come. I shouldn't have applied for the pageant in the first place.

Click and Leigh dug through the racks, chatting non-stop about fabrics and colors and asking the saleswoman about waistlines and hems and all sorts of stuff I didn't understand.

I fanned the bottom of my T-shirt as I moved toward the back of the store.

"That's our budget corner," the saleswoman called.

I ducked my head. She might as well have announced to the world that I couldn't afford any of the regular dresses. But Leigh joined me like shopping in the discount section was no big deal. She pulled out a dress that had an emerald green bottom and a white top that looked like a crocheted potholder from one of Mom's yard sales.

"Can you imagine wearing this?" Leigh asked.

I forced out a fake giggle. The dress was ugly, but according to the price tag, it was still way more expensive than I could ever afford.

The saleslady approached with her arms full of dresses. "Separate changing rooms?" she asked, leading us toward the back of the store.

"Yes, please," Leigh said, which was bold because I would have said one room so that we didn't take up any more space than we had to, even though we were the only ones here.

Everything in the waiting room was red and gold, and there was a spacious bench with scrolled edges. It looked more like a palace than a store in the mall.

The saleslady pulled aside a curtain and pointed at a little silver bell in the first stall. "Be sure to ring if you need me."

"I'll wait out here." Click pulled a book from her purse as she lowered herself to the bench.

Leigh bounced into the first fitting room. I wrinkled my nose as I entered the second. It smelled like stale perfume, cleaning products, and body odor—not like a palace at all.

"Which one are you going to try on first?" Leigh called from the room next to me.

"The black one, I guess." It was the shortest of the three the sales lady had picked out. It had thin straps, but it came with a little black jacket.

After changing, I inspected myself in the mirror. The jacket stuck out at a funny angle, and the color made me look like a zombie. I didn't think I had rings under my eyes, but the dress made it seem like I did.

"Let me see," Leigh called.

I pulled the curtains aside.

"Oh, my," Click said.

She tried to look positive, but her twitching lips told me everything I needed to know about this dress.

"Okay, well, I think we can rule this one out," she said. And then, to be encouraging, she added, "Sometimes it's just as helpful to know what doesn't work as it is to know what does."

I was about to dart back into my room when Leigh stepped out. Gauzy pink fabric softened her muscular body. If I didn't know better, I'd swear she was a movie star.

"What do you think?" She held her breath while waiting for my answer.

"You look like a million bucks."

She squealed and jumped up and down. Then she turned to her mom. "I know this is the first dress I've tried on, but I think it could be the one."

"You might be right," Click said. "Why don't you try on the others to be sure?"

Leigh disappeared back into her changing room. I pulled my curtains shut, eager to get this black dress of doom off my body.

I really didn't want to try on any more, but since Click and Leigh would have a fit if I didn't, I stepped into a red dress. A poufy skirt flared from a sequined band around the waist. It was the most ridiculous thing I'd ever seen, but as I pulled the top up to tie around my neck, something felt different. Even before looking in the mirror, I could tell the dress fit me perfectly.

When I turned around, a soft gasp escaped from my mouth. I'd been transformed from a trailer-living nobody into a real-life princess. The dress accented my curvy figure, and the color made my skin glow and my dark hair shine. I never imagined I could look this . . . pretty.

"You okay in there?" Click called.

I pushed the curtain aside.

"Fud," Click gasped. "You look extraordinary."

Heat rushed to my face.

Leigh, who was wearing a flowing lemon-colored dress that fit nicely but clashed with her complexion, clapped her hands and jumped up and down. "Fud," she said, "that's the one!"

My gaze flitted back to the mirror. I imagined the girl that smiled at me walking confidently across the stage. The crowd applauding enthusiastically. Someone placing a heavy crown on her head.

"Spin around," Click said. "Show us the back."

I did, and grew at least three inches taller when Click and Leigh gasped. "That's the one for sure," Click said.

Leigh crossed her arms and pretend-pouted. "How do you expect the rest of us to compete when you look like that?"

She meant it as a joke, but I darted back into the fitting room. After slipping out of the dress, I sank down on the plush footstool, clutching the red fabric in my lap. I wanted it so bad that my chest ached. The back of the price tag taunted me, daring me to look.

I forced a wobbly hand to flip it over.

I gasped.

There was no universe in which Mom could afford

this dress. My only hope was finding one at a second-hand store. But how would I win a pageant wearing someone's leftovers?

Cha-ching. Jackpot! Ava's mocking voice rang in my ears.

I jumped up and began dressing. It didn't matter. I probably wouldn't get into the stupid pageant anyway.

After returning the dress to its hanger, I left it behind and exited the fitting room.

Click eyed me. "You aren't going to try on the last dress?"

"I'm good." I sank onto the cushioned bench. Leigh stepped out. This time, she was in a black dress. It was strapless and tight all the way to the floor, where it flared out.

"Not bad," Click said. "But you were right; the first one was the winner." She pulled out her phone. "Let me snap a picture of the tag so we can track it down after you get your acceptance."

I blinked. She still hadn't checked the price. And there was no talk of layaway or coming back when it was on sale.

I tried to squash a swell of anger. It wasn't Leigh's fault she didn't have to worry about money. Still, I wondered if she knew how lucky she was.

From inside her dressing room, she handed out the pink dress. Click snapped a picture and then turned to me. "Should we get a picture of your tag, too?"

"Oh," I said. "Sure. I guess that's a good idea."

I'd been optimistic about getting into the pageant earlier, but now I was sure there was a better chance of a comet hitting Earth.

"I can hardly believe it," Leigh said, coming out of her fitting room and linking her arm through mine. "We both found our dresses on the same day!"

I wished I could share her enthusiasm, but another wave of resentment swelled inside me. It wasn't that I wanted her to have it harder, and I didn't want her to know how I was feeling, but I wished things could be a little easier for me every once in a while, too.

"What's next?" Click asked.

"Let's look for shoes," Leigh said, skipping ahead.

I was ready to ditch the mall, but I shuffled behind her.

Bright light shined on an enormous display in the front of the shoe store, highlighting heels I was certain no human could balance in.

"Can I help you?" A tall, Black saleswoman with natural hair approached us. She brought with her the scent of cherry licorice. Her flashy suit was paired with the highest sequined heels I'd ever seen, and she didn't wobble one bit.

"We're looking for pageant shoes," Click said.

"My name is Imani." The saleswoman flashed a

bright smile. "I'd be pleased to help you with that. Follow me."

She spun around and sauntered toward the back of the room, walking like a supermodel. Customer's heads swiveled to follow her, but she didn't seem to notice. I couldn't imagine being that comfortable in my skin. Not caring that I was the center of attention.

Maybe it'd be easy if I looked as good as she did. But I had a feeling that even if she were in wrinkled pajamas, she'd still turn the heads of everyone in the room.

"Are you coming?" Leigh asked.

I hurried to catch up, grateful that by now, the rest of the customers had gone back to their own business. We stopped at a bank of soft stools. I wiped my sweaty palms on my pants, reminding myself no one here knew I could never afford these shoes. All I had to do was pretend, same as I did with Larry when he cracked one of his stupid jokes.

Imani motioned toward the shelves behind us. "We'll start here. First, tell me about your dresses."

I nodded for Leigh to go ahead.

After listening carefully, Imani held up a finger. Her long nails were painted in a black-and-white checkered pattern. "I know just the shoe," she said. "What size are you?"

"Five and a half," Leigh said.

"I'll be right back." Imani returned with a dainty

pair of heels that had delicate butterflies perched on the straps.

Leigh squealed. "Those are perfect!"

Imani flashed us a bright smile. "What can I say? I'm good at what I do."

Some people were definitely born with a fashion gene. She turned to me. "Now, let's get you taken care of."

"Oh no, no shoes for me. Not today."

Leigh grabbed my hand. "Come on, you've got to at least try some on. It'll be fun."

She wasn't going to let this go. And maybe it would be a little bit fun. I'd never worn heels before.

"I'm sure we can find the right pair," Imani said. "Why don't you tell me about your dress?"

"Um, well, it's red." She needed more of a description, but she was so polished and put together and perfect. My tongue refused to move off the roof of my mouth.

Leigh jumped in. "It's ruby red, and it's a halter top with a flared skirt . . ."

Listening to her describe the dress only made my tongue stick more firmly to the roof of my mouth. How did she *know* all these things?

Imani asked Leigh a few more questions and addressed me again. "What size are you?"

"Oh, um . . ." My mind spun like the tires on The Miracle the time we'd gotten it stuck in a snowbank. I had no idea what size my sneakers were—Mom had picked them up at a yard sale over the summer. "I'm not sure."

Imani stepped back and crooked her head, studying my worn tennis shoes. Mom said I had Flintstone feet because they were square and flat. She also said I came by them honestly, which didn't make any sense at all because how could anyone come by their feet dishonestly?

"Let's start with a seven and go from there," Imani said. "I know just the shoe."

She disappeared into the back.

"Don't Worry, Be Happy" played from inside Click's purse. She dug out her phone and glanced at the screen. "It's a gallery," she said, heading toward another corner of the store. "I need to take this."

Muffled giggles came from the next aisle, accompanied by a voice I recognized. *Uh-oh.* Footsteps drew near. Ava Benson came into view.

"Hi!" she said. I couldn't tell if she was surprised to see us or not.

"Hi." Leigh's cheeks flamed red.

She was probably embarrassed to be seen with me. Riding the bus to and from school was one thing, but hanging out with me on weekends was like walking around with a Loser sign hung around her neck.

"What are you doing here?" Ava asked.

"Shopping for pageant shoes," Leigh said.

"*Both* of you?" Ava arched an eyebrow.

Her friends snickered.

Heat didn't just creep up my neck, it made my face burn so hot I half expected smoke to start coming out my ears.

"Of course both of us." Leigh smiled, completely oblivious to the insult Ava had lobbed my way. "Fud applied to the pageant too, remember?"

"Oh, right. My bad," Ava said, smirking.

Now the heat built behind my eyes.

A well-dressed lady I assumed was Ava's mom called to her from the front of the store.

"Gotta run," Ava said, making eye contact with Leigh and ignoring me. "See you later."

I busied myself by pulling off a shoe and a sock, then froze. Dark tufts of hair sprouted from the knuckles in my toes, making it look like I was part hobbit. I darted a panicked glance at Leigh to see if she'd noticed. Thankfully, she was watching Ava's group leave the store.

A bolt of energy shot through me, like I'd been plugged into an electrical socket. Trembling, I yanked my sock back on. First my eyebrows, now this. I'd noticed a lot more hair under my arms lately, too. My whole body had apparently developed a mind of its own.

Imani returned with a box. "I found the perfect pair for you."

Leigh peeked inside. Her eyes widened. "Those are stunning!"

She clapped her hands and spun toward me. "Fud, they'll be gorgeous with your dress!"

"She's right," Click said, rejoining us. "They'll be a perfect match."

The shoes *would* be perfect for the dress. The toes were open, but a panel of jewels stretched up toward the ankle. I imagined myself clicking across the stage in them. Then I imagined everyone staring at my shaggy toes.

"I changed my mind," I said, trying to hide my shaking hands as I pulled on my shoe. "I don't feel like trying them on right now."

"You *have* to try them," Leigh said.

"I have to get home. Mom said I couldn't stay long," I lied.

Confusion flashed across Leigh's face, followed by disappointment.

"That gives you a good excuse to come back soon," Imani said.

Leigh brightened. "Good point. We could make a day of it and get pedicures, too."

I stiffened. It couldn't be coincidence that she mentioned a pedicure right after I'd taken off my socks.

"I knew you were my kind of girls." Imani beamed.

"Hey, I want in on the pedicure action, too," Click said, grinning.

They continued bantering. The tips of my ears burned as I studied Leigh's face. But there was nothing in her gaze to make me think she knew anything about my disgusting toes.

I breathed a deep sigh of relief as I followed her out of the store.

CHAPTER NINE

Days and then weeks passed without any word from the pageant. The boat was now cleaned up, painted bright red, and had a deck as well as a cabin framed in over a couple of holding tanks Larry said were for water and waste. Despite the progress, his behavior was as unpredictable as the fall weather. Some days, he was reasonable. Other days, he raged about everything from his truck to money to imagined slights, as though Mom went around chipping dishes on purpose. He hadn't hit her again, but it seemed only a matter of time.

Leigh refused to check her email at school because she was worried about having a public meltdown if she didn't get in. Since I'd used her email address, I raced home with her every day, where we flung ourselves on her bed, squeezed our eyes shut, and built up the courage to open her email.

"They've got to tell us any day," she said, tumbling onto her bed one crisp afternoon in the middle of September. "The pageant is next month."

I sank down next to her and held my breath as she unlocked her phone.

"Omgomgomgomgomg," she yelled, popping up and running in place.

"What is it?" I asked, sitting up straight. "Tell me!"

"This is it. Two emails from the pageant."

My stomach twisted like a wet dish towel. So far, I'd avoided thinking about what would happen if Leigh got in and I didn't. She and Ava were shoo-ins, but the pageant committee—or whoever made the decision— would surely see right through my photos and stamp a bright red REJECT across my application.

Leigh tossed the phone on the bed like it was radioactive.

"What are you doing?" I asked. "Read it!"

"I can't." She wrapped her arms around herself. "What if I'm rejected?"

The idea was so ridiculous that I snorted and grabbed the phone. "If you aren't going to check, then I will."

I tapped on the email with her name in the subject line.

"Don't read it," she shrieked, covering her face. "No, read it. Just don't tell me if I didn't get in."

While she was carrying on, I read the letter.

Dear Everleigh,
The Powder River Basin Coal Mine is pleased to inform

you that your application to participate in the upcoming Miss Tween Black Gold pageant has been accepted. The pageant . . .

"You're in," I said.

"What?"

"You're in!"

One hand clapped over her mouth. Tears sparkled in her eyes. "I can't be. I don't believe it. Let me see!"

I tipped the phone toward her. She scanned the screen. Her smile was bright enough to fry an egg. I wondered why the pageant meant so much to her, but before I had time to ask, she looked up. "Do you want to open yours or do you want me to?"

I bit my lip. Opening her letter hadn't been any big deal, but now that she was in, I wasn't sure I wanted to open mine.

I picked at the edge of the plastic screen protector.

"There's really no point," I said, blinking quickly. "There's no way we both got in."

Leigh grabbed the phone. "Don't be a doofus. If I got in, then you *definitely* got in."

She was just being nice.

She poked at the screen and started reading. I steeled myself. I wouldn't cry. I wouldn't.

"Dear Felicity, the Powder River Basin Coal Mine is pleased to inform you . . ."

She dropped the phone to her side. "You're in! We're both in!"

I was in? I grabbed the phone from her, needing to see for myself. I was in! Adrenaline raced through me. We gripped hands and jumped up and down, shrieking.

Click poked her head in the door. "Everything okay in here?"

"We're both in the pageant!" Leigh said.

Click beamed. "I'm not one bit surprised."

Leigh danced around the room. "Next stop, dress town!"

"Should we hit the mall this weekend?" Click asked.

"Perfect!" Leigh said. "We can pick up shoes then, too. Are you free, Fud?"

I was definitely not free for another mall trip. "My mom will probably want to take me."

"We can go together," Leigh said. "It'll be a mother-daughter double date!"

I scrambled for an excuse. "Maybe. I'm not sure Mom will be able to make it this weekend. She hasn't been feeling great lately."

Leigh was about to say something when Click cut in.

"I'm sorry to hear that. I'd be glad to bring over a pot of soup, or if there's anything I can do to lend a hand . . ."

"She'll be fine," I said. "It's probably only a head cold."

"We're here if she needs help with anything. The same goes for you."

"Thanks." I dropped my gaze to the carpet. It was nice of her to offer, but it wasn't as if I could ask for the kind of help I needed.

I wanted to tell Mom about the pageant, but she didn't come out of her room for dinner. Larry made us grilled cheese sandwiches, but he burned one side. Even after scraping the burned part off with the edge of a butter knife, they were hardly edible. I choked mine down and spent the evening in my room arranging a collection of shark's teeth I'd found up on the ridge. Larry had showed me where to search for them back when we first moved in and he was still pretending to be a nice guy.

My stomach felt a bit like one of the sharks was thrashing around inside it, searching for its lost tooth. It had been several weeks since Mom first got sick, and she seemed to be getting worse, not better. I read a book once about a kid whose Mom acted the same way— turned out, she had cancer and died three months later.

I bit my knuckle.

Mom couldn't die. Spending the rest of my life alone with Larry was more than I could bear. I jumped up from my raft and rushed to her bedroom. Deep, even breaths wafted from under the closed door. I lifted my hand to knock, then let it drop again. If she was sleeping, I didn't want to bother her. And if she was awake . . . either she would be fine and I was overreacting or she really was going to die, and I wasn't ready to face that yet. I wouldn't be ready to face that *ever*.

I rested my forehead against the doorframe, wishing I was a little girl again so I could fling open the door and run into the room. I'd spring into her bed and snuggle in her arms. "Felicity means happiness," she'd whisper. "I picked that name because that's what you brought into my life."

I trudged back to my room, slipped the teeth in the pickle jar I stored them in, and set it on my makeshift nightstand. I tried to force myself to think about the pageant, but that didn't help. What good would it do to win if Mom wasn't around? There was no denying she looked terrible. She'd lost weight and seemed more run-down than The Miracle, which was really saying something.

When I finally dozed off, my sleep was restless. That changed near dawn, when I fell into the comfort of a dream. In it, I had a bird's-eye view of a familiar mother coyote watching proudly as five pups engaged in a ferocious wrestling match to establish dominance.

After several minutes, the biggest and strongest pup claimed his role as leader. A second pup, obviously intelligent and scrappy, took her place beside her brother as second-in-command. I was studying the three remaining pups when a sixth sense warned me of danger.

I scanned the horizon and found a mountain lion slinking toward the coyotes. *Run*, I wanted to yell. *Hide!*

But I had no body, no voice. I could only hover anxiously nearby as the mountain lion neared.

Moments before it pounced, the mother coyote sat up and let out a short, sharp bark. Her pups startled and dove for the den. Before the last one was inside, the mountain lion was on the mother, its teeth sunk into her neck.

They rolled over and over. I wanted to look away but couldn't. Grunts and yowls came from the pair as their bodies wrenched apart. They circled each other, the mountain lion crouching as if preparing to pounce, the coyote bleeding but determined to stand her ground.

A much larger coyote appeared out of nowhere. Its teeth sank into the lion's fur. The lion howled. Two more coyotes joined in the fight. The mountain lion was agile and muscular, but it was no match for a pack of angry coyotes. It tried to run away, but the largest coyote caught it by the hind leg and dragged it back. Again and again the coyotes attacked, not stopping until the mountain lion lay lifeless on the ground. My heart thundered in my ears as the largest coyote licked blood from the mother's fur. They'd done it! The coyotes had protected the pups!

I blinked awake, my heart pounding as though I'd been one of the coyotes in the fight. Instead of feeling sorry for the mountain lion, I felt . . . admiration for the coyotes. Most people thought they were cowardly. Some indigenous cultures viewed them as tricksters.

Either way, they were smart enough to stay away from humans. More important, they protected their own. Any one of those coyotes would have given its life to protect the pups.

My thoughts were interrupted by puking sounds coming from the bathroom. Larry would have already left for work. I jumped out of bed.

"Are you okay?" I yelled through the bathroom door.

"I will be," Mom croaked.

When I was sick, she always made me oatmeal and tea. I went to the kitchen and started some water boiling. I was spooning the thick, gloppy oatmeal into bowls when she padded into the kitchen.

She sank down at the table. "Good morning."

I set a bowl of oatmeal in front of her. The bruise around her eye had long since faded, but her hair was stringy and there were dark circles under her eyes. The shark started swimming around in my stomach again. "Maybe you should see a doctor?"

"Larry says doctors are quacks."

Mom had taken me to doctors to get my vaccinations plenty of times when I was younger, and they'd all seemed fine to me. This was probably an excuse so Larry didn't have to pay for one. When I won the pageant, I'd book Mom an appointment first thing.

"Anyway, I don't need a doctor yet," Mom said, stirring her oatmeal. "This comes with the territory."

Yet?

She *was* sick. My insides simmered like a pot of boiling oatmeal. I wanted to know how bad it was, but I couldn't bring myself to ask.

"It's been a while since we caught up," Mom said, making an effort to sound perky. "What's new? Tell me everything."

I took a deep breath. The pageant was more important now than ever.

"Leigh and I both got into the Miss Tween Black Gold Pageant," I said, watching her closely.

"Oh yeah?" She reached for her tea.

My shoulders sagged. I'd hoped for a little more enthusiasm.

I decided to try again. "Hundreds of girls probably applied, but only thirty of us were selected."

"When is it?"

"October sixteenth. At the convention center."

She blew on the tea, trying to cool it. "You know I'm not going to be able to give you a ride."

I stirred my oatmeal. The old mom would have been proud of me. But that was back when she'd been the leader of our pack. Before she'd given up the spot to Larry. Before she got sick.

My stomach churned with anger. Frustration. Sadness. Fear. I remembered my dream. How fierce the coyotes had been, protecting their own. How they wouldn't have given up, no matter what. I had to do the same. No more shy, hesitant Fud. Getting into the pageant wasn't enough. I had to *win*.

I always paid careful attention during announcements because I didn't want to miss anything that might make me look stupid later (like the time the principal announced that we could ignore the fire alarms because they were being tested, and I was the only one who jumped out of my chair when they went off).

But I sat up especially straight when the principal congratulated the three girls from our school who had been accepted into the Miss Tween Black Gold Pageant. As he babbled about how he expected the participants to represent the school with honor, my mind twisted faster than a tornado.

Only three girls from our school had made it in? Who was the third girl? *Please not Ava Benson* played on repeat in my mind as he talked.

"Please, everyone take the time to congratulate Felicity Dahlers, Everleigh Jaffa, and Ava Benson."

I slumped in my seat. Of course Ava had gotten in.

But I didn't have time to think too much about that, because applause filled the air. One of my classmates whistled.

Heat rushed to my face. Since when did any of these kids care about anything I did?

When the principal finished speaking, my homeroom teacher, Ms. José-Fitzgerald, smiled. She was a petite woman who had grown up in Honduras but moved to the States for college. She was my favorite teacher, not only because she taught science, but also because she never acted like my cruddy clothes meant I couldn't be trusted to get my work done or that I was dumber than the other kids. "It appears we have a celebrity right here in class. Congratulations, Fud. I'm sure you'll do us proud."

I gave her a half-hearted smile. I didn't care one bit about doing them proud—I only wanted to save Mom. I picked at the edge of my desk, wishing the bell would ring so we could start first period.

"How did *she* get in?" one of Ava Benson's groupies fake whispered.

"She gets all her clothes used," another one said, giggling.

"You're just jealous," a boy named Lamonte said, shutting them up. Lamonte and I used to play tetherball together at recess in elementary school, but his mom made him stop after he got a concussion in gym class.

Tyler snickered. "She's got the chest for it."

I crossed my arms.

"Tyler, is there something you want to share with the class?" Ms. José-Fitzgerald asked.

"Nope. Just congratulating Fud on the pageant."

I stared at my desk, hoping Ms. José-Fitzgerald wouldn't keep pushing.

Even after we pulled out our notebooks and began our science lesson, I had the feeling that everyone in class kept sneaking glances at me.

This went on all morning. On my way to the library for lunch, I was stopped by another teacher, Ms. Finley. I didn't have any classes with her this year, but last year she was my language arts teacher, and I liked her okay, even if she did wear too much makeup and got overly excited about weird things like Oxford commas.

"Fud," she said, beaming. Makeup caked the wrinkles at the corners of her clear blue eyes. Bright lipstick contrasted with her tanned skin. "I'm delighted about the pageant. Congratulations."

"Thank you," I said, tucking my head and scuffing my toes.

"I was thinking you and the other girls might need some guidance."

I frowned. "Guidance?"

"You know, how to walk, prepping for the interview, that sort of thing."

"Oh, um . . ."

"I was Miss Tween Black Gold back in my day, you know."

I tried to imagine Ms. Finley in a crown and sash.

She laughed. "I know," she said, using her hands to

draw attention to the lumpy body she hid behind a baggy dress and a chunky zebra-inspired necklace, "it's hard to imagine, but it's true. I cut quite the figure once upon a time."

Hope trickled into my chest like water from a faucet. If I was going to stand any chance of winning, I needed all the help I could get. "That'd be great."

Ms. Finley clasped her hands together at her chest. "I'm so happy you agreed. Ava and Leigh said yes, too. I have lunch duty this quarter, but I can find someone to cover me for a day. Meet me in my classroom next Monday."

Wait a minute. I'd agreed to spend an entire lunch hour with Ava Benson?

The shark in my stomach took a giant bite. I groaned, wishing it would swallow me whole.

CHAPTER TEN

Monday morning, I woke up exhausted from another night filled with coyote dreams. I didn't know what my recent obsession was about—even though it was amazing that they could control their litter size depending on how much food was around, coyotes weren't my favorite animal. That honor went to the bison.

They were the largest land animals in North America, and the hump on their back was actually muscle, which they needed to support their heads as they plowed snow out of the way. There were plenty of things—or people—I'd plow through if I had that kind of strength.

Not even my worries about today's pageant practice with Ms. Finley could keep me from letting out a giant yawn in science, which I tried to hide behind my hand.

Luckily, Ms. José-Fitzgerald announced that we were taking a break from studying organisms to discuss current events. I sat up straight when she started with a recent experiment to combine human and animal cells. I didn't know that kind of thing was possible. Apparently all of the experiments, which happened in petri dishes, had ended in failure.

Ms. José-Fitzgerald wanted to discuss the moral and ethical implications of growing animal-human hybrids, but I was more interested in the science. I'd read about coyotes and wolves mating and producing something called coywolves. But those two animals were closely related. Ms. José-Fitzgerald said these sorts of things were carefully regulated, and I couldn't imagine the government allowing actual animal-human hybrids.

The class moved on. I kept myself awake by doodling coyote-human hybrids. Then I moved on to bear, big-horn sheep, and elk-human hybrids. They all looked ridiculous.

By lunchtime, I was a bundle of nerves. Luckily, Ms. Finley's room was set up exactly the same as last year, complete with quotes from her favorite books all over the walls. When I stepped inside, she interrupted the story she'd been telling Ava and Leigh. "You're here!"

"Unfortunately," Ava muttered under her breath. Her lilac scent filled my nose.

"Back at you," I mumbled, deciding I hated the smell of lilacs. Right away, I felt stupid. We were too old to trade insults like little kids. *Don't let her get under your skin,* I reminded myself. But Ava was sitting in a desk in the front row, looking every bit as perfect as always in jeans, Converse shoes, and an off-the-shoulder sweater that highlighted her layered necklaces. I wanted to wipe the fake smile right off her face.

"Let's get started," Miss Finley said. "All three of you are already beautiful. But the judges are looking for more than beauty. They're looking for perfection, outside and in."

If perfection was what they wanted, then perfection was what I'd give them.

Ms. Finley handed us a stack of papers, explaining that these were some of the topics we might be asked about during the interview portion of the pageant. "If you want to win, you'll need to show up prepared."

Ava grumbled about the homework, but I was happy for the help.

"The pageant is in four weeks. We have a lot to cover if you're going to be ready. Let's start by practicing your walks." Ms. Finley rose from her desk and straightened the large pearls that seemed like overkill with her frilly shirt and thick blazer.

"What for?" I asked, slipping into a desk next to Leigh. "I've been walking my whole life."

Ava rolled her eyes. "Our *runway* walks."

Ms. Finley shifted the desks to create a little more space down one of the aisles and invited us to stand up. "The way you walk onstage tells the judge all about you. Confident, spicy, shy—it all comes through."

She walked down the aisle, but the way she moved made it almost seem like she was floating. The transformation reminded me of a polar bear cam I'd been obsessed with in fourth grade. The bear had been big and bulky out of the water, but in the pool, it had been as smooth and graceful as a ballerina.

"Gliding tells the judges you're poised and elegant." She changed the way she walked by lifting her knees higher and bringing her feet down with more force. "A spirited walk tells them you've got energy and drive."

"Which walk tells them you're poor?" Ava whispered to Leigh.

Leigh's eyebrows drew together. I waited for her to tell Ava to knock it off, but she didn't say anything. She was probably too focused on Ms. Finley to bother.

"Everyone's body is different," Ms. Finley said, "and everyone's walk is different, too—you've got to find the one that works *for* you, not *against* you. Now come on, show me what you've got. Ava, you're up first."

Ava gave us a catlike smile. "Look and learn, girls."

She smoothed her skinny jeans. Watching her sail down the aisle, I was tempted to groan. Of course she could already walk like a model. At the other end she spun, placed a hand on her hip, and smiled sweetly. "Your turn, Leigh."

"Wish me luck," Leigh said.

"Good luck," I said automatically.

Not that she needed it. Her walk was more spirited than Ava's, making the small bells on her furry boots tinkle, but it was nearly as polished. Ms. Finley had her do it two more times with her chin up. When Leigh got back to Ava, Ava clapped and squealed. "That was great!"

"Do you think so?" Leigh asked.

"Definitely," Ava said.

Leigh smiled bashfully. I raised my eyebrows. Leigh hadn't mentioned Ava in weeks. I'd figured that meant she'd seen for herself what kind of person Ava was.

"You're both ready to practice in heels," Ms. Finley said. "Fud, let's see what you're made of."

Ava snorted.

I wiped my sweaty palms on my jeans. Showing the judges the real me was the last thing I wanted to do. Ms. Finley, Leigh, and Ava waited.

My empty stomach grumbled.

"Go ahead," Ms. Finley said. "Let your inner spirit shine."

I started moving down the aisle, swaying my hips back and forth as I attempted to glide.

"Okay, that's a start," Ms. Finley said when I finished.

Ava's hand flew to her mouth to hide her smirk.

Leigh's mouth twitched.

I wanted to disappear.

Ms. Finley motioned for me to go again. "This time, keep your hips still. The movement should come from your legs."

I'd been exaggerating my hip movement on purpose. No wonder I'd looked ridiculous.

"Stand up straight, core tight, shoulders back," Ms. Finley called. "Chin up."

"Better!" she said after I'd finished. "Much better. One more time, but I want you to really exaggerate your leg movements."

I felt ridiculous lifting my legs higher, stretching them out, and plunking them down with more force, but I could tell by the surprised look on Ava's face that I was doing it right. "Easy peasy," I said when I reached her.

"That was great!" Leigh squeezed my arm.

"Whatever," Ava mumbled.

I could barely hide my grin.

"Now we're going to practice our pivot turns," Ms. Finley said.

I paid close attention while she demonstrated. *Stop, pivot, start walking with front foot.*

I could do this!

"Leigh, let's start with you this time. Do your walk down here, execute a pivot turn, and walk back."

Leigh walked, pivoted, and started to return, but Ms. Finley stopped her for a correction.

Ava leaned close and whispered in my ear. "What's wrong with her?"

A silent growl built inside me. "What do you mean— nothing's wrong with her."

"There must be. Otherwise why would she hang out with *you*?" Ava whispered.

The smell of wet dog filled my nose. My body tingled, and I was overcome with the sudden urge to tackle Ava. "Shut your mouth."

"Have you hit any jackpots lately?" she asked, smiling cruelly.

Hot rage coursed through me. My vision tunneled until I saw only Ava's sneering face. I snarled and lunged toward her, knocking us both to the carpet. Her mouth was open, but I didn't hear anything coming out. She threw up her hands to protect her face from my flailing fists.

I opened my own mouth, determined to clamp down on her bare arm. Before my teeth pierced her soft skin, someone yanked me from behind. I flailed, determined to keep fighting. To make her pay for every cruel word she'd ever said.

Ms. Finley pulled me to my feet and wrapped her arms around me until I stilled. My vision cleared, and my hearing, which had disappeared during the fight, returned in a rush.

Ava was curled on the floor, sobbing.

"What were you thinking?" Leigh yelled. Both her hands were on her head like she couldn't believe what she'd witnessed.

My head spun.

Ms. Finley, who was panting heavily, loosened her arms. "Go to the office," she said. "Now."

Ava's gaze met mine.

I gasped like she'd socked me in the gut. The look in her eyes was the same one I must have had when Larry stuffed my face in the sink.

I backed up, stumbling over a desk.

"Did you hear me?" Ms. Finley said. "To the office."

Leigh's eyes burned into my back as I ran from the room.

The smell of lilacs followed me as I sprinted down the school's main hall. Instead of turning left into the office, I turned right, crossed the lobby, and pushed my way out the front door.

I wasn't sure what I was planning—to run all the way back to Larry's trailer, maybe, but the cold air slapped some sense into me. I descended the stairs and paced back and forth on the sidewalk, trying to calm myself down. My pulse raced and my knees threatened to give out. I'd actually attacked someone!

She deserved it, a voice inside me said.

That didn't mean you had to go all wild animal on her, Mom's voice argued.

In kindergarten, I'd told Mom how a kid named Joachim had kicked another kid for making fun of him. I hadn't thought there was anything wrong with Joachim defending himself, but Mom had explained that violence was only acceptable if I was defending myself from physical harm.

She obviously didn't know that words could hurt just as badly.

I kicked a pebble. It tumbled down the sidewalk and came to a rest, stuck waiting there until someone came along and kicked it again. I wanted to believe that my attack had been justified, but I knew exactly what it was like to be on the receiving end of someone's anger. And I couldn't get the scared look in Ava's eyes out of my mind.

If Ms. Finley hadn't stopped me, I would have bitten Ava. A small part of me still wanted to. The metallic taste of blood seemed to fill my mouth. Instead of horrifying me, it only made my stomach rumble with hunger. That was messed up. *I* was messed up. I cringed. Maybe Ava had been right about me all along.

I figured I'd wait outside until the buses arrived, but a half hour later the woman Ava had been with at the mall rushed into the school clutching her purse like she expected someone to snatch it any second. Larry's beat-up truck rumbled down the street a heartbeat later.

Uh-oh. I almost dashed back inside—I'd rather face whatever punishment the principal doled out than Larry's anger. But if I was in trouble now, that'd be nothing compared to running away from Larry after he'd left work to pick me up. I moved toward the truck with heavy steps, realizing I'd left my jacket and backpack inside. Whatever. All that stuff would still be there tomorrow.

The truck door sometimes stuck, so I tugged extra hard to get it open. I climbed in the cab. Larry's work overalls smelled like decomposing garbage. Empty beer cans, dirty rags, and miscellaneous tools littered the cab. I pulled the door shut.

"You know how hard it was for me to get out of work?" Larry's voice dripped with venom.

I tucked my head and focused on a crushed fast-food wrapper, waiting for him to continue. He chewed on a straw as he put the truck in gear and pulled away from the curb. He still hadn't said another word by the time we reached the highway a few minutes later. I guessed he was trying to work out the best punishment for me.

"Thanks for the ride," I finally said, hoping to soften him up.

"That old windbag of a principal didn't exactly give me a choice." He drummed his thumb on the steering wheel.

"What do you mean?"

"They said I had to come pick you up."

My hands squeezed into fists. I would rather have sat outside forever than get picked up by Larry.

He continued. "They want to have some big meeting in the morning to discuss disciplinary measures. I told her where she could stick her meeting and her disciplinary measures and said they should let kids be kids, but she's a real know-it-all. Thinks she's better than me because she sits behind a fancy desk."

I'd seen the principal's desk once when I was in the office delivering a note for a teacher. The dull brown metal had been covered in dents.

I squirmed, wondering what kind of "disciplinary measures" they gave kids like me. Detention? Suspension? I hoped not—I couldn't keep up with my classes if I wasn't in school. Then again, if they kicked me out I wouldn't have to see Ava Benson again anytime soon.

Larry cranked down his window, letting in a rush of cold air.

"The whole system is a joke," he said, tossing out his straw.

My jaw clenched, but I didn't dare lecture him for littering.

He rolled his window up. "When we're on the boat, you can homeschool. Then you won't have to worry about those losers."

I sucked in deep breaths, trying to keep myself from vomiting all over Larry and his pickup. Suddenly, his littering felt like the least of my problems.

I'd mostly gotten myself under control when the dumpster marking our turnoff came into sight, and we slowed.

"So what does the other guy look like?" Larry pulled the truck onto our gravel road.

"Huh?"

"You don't seem to be hurt, so I'm wondering what the other guy looks like."

He grinned like this whole thing was a joke.

I remembered the look on Ava's face. "Not great."

"Atta girl!" Larry held out his fist to bump.

Reluctantly, I held up my own fist.

"Did you work in an uppercut?"

"Uh, I'm not sure." I didn't want to go over the fight with him, but at the same time, I couldn't believe this. He wasn't just *not mad*—he was *happy* I'd pummeled Ava.

"Did you at least protect your thumbs?"

When we first moved in with Larry and he'd still been trying to impress Mom with what a good guy he was, he'd given me boxing lessons. He'd showed me how to form a fist with my thumbs on the outside so I didn't break them when I punched someone. At the time, I hadn't thought it was a tip I'd ever need. But I must have protected my thumbs when I'd hit Ava. "Good as new," I said, holding up my hands.

"Maybe there's hope for you yet."

His words made me sit up taller. I wasn't proud of what I'd done, but if I could stand up to Ava Benson, then there was hope that I'd be able to stand up to the guy sitting next to me when the time came.

CHAPTER ELEVEN

Larry zoomed back to work as soon as he dropped me off. Mom was sleeping when I went inside, so I spent the afternoon in my room. Around the time school got out, I slid on Mom's jacket and went outside to sit on the tractor. While I waited for the bus, I pretended to steer down the road and onto the highway, where the tractor would carry Mom and me to our next apartment.

I was worried about seeing Leigh, but I needed to know how mad she was. I got my answer as soon as she stepped off the bus and spotted me waiting. Heaving her backpack over her shoulder, she stormed toward me, making the bells on her boots clang.

"What were you thinking?" Her eyes shone with fury.

I'd figured she'd be upset, but I'd also thought she'd at least give me a chance to explain. My own anger swelled inside me. "I was *thinking* it was time that rat got what she deserved."

"You think she deserved to be attacked? For what? For teasing you?"

"It was a lot more than teasing, and you know it."

She crossed her arms. "I don't care what it was. You can't go around beating up people because you don't like how they treat you."

I cringed. Leigh would really freak if she knew how close I'd come to biting Ava. "I shouldn't have lost it, okay? But don't pretend she didn't deserve something." Leigh was supposed to be my *friend*—she was supposed to have my back. My eyes narrowed. "Why are you defending her?"

"I'm not defending her," Leigh said. "But she's not a monster."

"How can you say that?" Now I crossed my arms. "She makes fun of me *all the time*. About everything. She *is* a monster."

"That's not true. I have math with her. She can actually be really nice sometimes."

The faint scent of lilacs wafted toward me. Leigh raised a hand to her mouth and chewed on a thumbnail.

"How can you still like her?" I spat. "You've seen how she treats me."

Leigh shrugged and gazed off in the distance. "I know she can be awful, but she's been helping me with my math homework. She's smart and really funny."

"I can't believe this." I jumped down from the tractor. "You have a crush on the meanest girl in school."

"It's not a crush! It's just . . . she's pretty, that's all."

If Leigh were really my friend, she'd see how nasty Ava was. I got up in her face. "Pretty and smart and funny and nice. Sounds like a crush to me."

"Look, it's not like I'm planning to date her or anything."

I wondered how long this had been going on. "How come you didn't tell me?"

Leigh shrugged. "It's not that big of a deal. She doesn't like me back. Plus, I knew you'd be mad."

"I'm not mad," I growled. "But you're smart, and pretty, and your life is perfect—you could pick anyone at school you wanted. Why did you have to pick Ava Benson?"

Leigh exploded. "I didn't *pick* anyone. And if you think my life is perfect, then you don't know me at all."

She marched toward her trailer without glancing back.

She had no idea what real problems felt like. "What?" I yelled. "Did you get a ninety-eight instead of a ninety-nine in math? Or let me guess, your mom bought you the wrong color shirt? The wrong flavor of chips? You really think I should feel sorry for you? You need to wake up."

Leigh stopped and clenched her fists.

She spun to face me. "Maybe you're right," she spat. "Maybe I do need to wake up. Because all this time, I thought you were my friend."

She sprinted away, kicking up a cloud of dust.

I stormed past our trailer. I couldn't bring myself to go inside and face a lecture from Mom. When I reached the top of the bluff, a movement on the plain below caught my eye. A coyote. I squinted, trying to figure out if it was one I'd seen before, but something was wrong with my eyes. I could see details fine, but the world had lost its color. Everything had turned dull shades of gray except the sky, which was tinged blue. I tried to blink everything back to normal, but it didn't work.

A short animal with a long, sturdy body shuffled beside the coyote, capturing my attention. Even with whatever was going on with my eyes, I could still make out a lighter stripe running from its nose over its shoulders. What in the world was a badger doing with a coyote?

The two animals strolled side by side. Without warning, the badger started pawing the ground, sending dirt flying. The coyote jogged several feet away and paused with its head down.

A small animal popped up from the ground under the coyote. The coyote pounced. When it rose again, a kangaroo rat dangled from its mouth, hind legs squirming and kicking. A few seconds later, the badger stopped digging. When it turned to leave, a rat hung from its mouth as well.

I watched, too stunned to move, until both animals disappeared into the distance. Then I blinked several times. My vision sorted itself, and color returned to the world. I squinted at the bright blue sky, feeling like someone had flipped on the light in a dark room. I had no idea what that was about, but I didn't much care—I'd just witnessed something amazing. Maybe something no other human had ever seen before!

I couldn't wait to get back to school to search the internet. But as I approached the trailer, I slowed. It was probably better if I told Mom about the fight before she found out from Larry.

I opened the door and let out a surprised squeak. Mom was on her hands and knees, sorting long strands of rope that ran from the front of the living room to the back of the kitchen. Macramé. This was actually good news.

"You're feeling better?"

"Seems that way." She leaned back on her heels.

I fought a swell of tears. I hadn't realized how much her illness had been weighing on me.

She brushed a strand of hair from her face. "You want to tell me what's going on?"

My stomach knotted like Mom's rope was tangled inside me. She'd obviously heard my fight with Leigh.

"It's nothing," I said. "Just a little trouble at school."

"Trouble at school is not nothing. Spit it out," Mom said, placing her hands on her hips. "What happened?"

I told her everything except the part about how I'd almost bitten Ava. And I left out the meeting in the morning—Larry had made it clear he thought it was stupid, and I didn't want to give him and Mom anything to fight about.

When I finished explaining, Mom let out a deep, disappointed breath. "You know fighting is never the answer. You're better than that. Smarter than that."

I hung my head.

She sighed and climbed to her feet. Sinking down on the couch, she patted the cushion beside her. "I know what it's like to lose it. To make decisions you regret."

I curled up next to her.

"I don't want you to end up like me. I want so much better for you. That can only happen if you stay on the straight and narrow, you understand?"

I kind of understood. I wanted better for me, too. And for her.

She put her arm around me and pulled me close. I leaned into her bony shoulder. "What decisions do you regret?"

She let out a small, sad laugh. "How much time do you have?"

I was sure one of them must be Larry. But in her mind, we were drowning and he was the only lifeboat in sight. This was my chance to fix things for her. For us.

I cleared my throat. "So the pageant is next month."

"That's right," Mom said. "How are you feeling about that?"

"I'll need a dress to compete."

She didn't respond, so I rushed ahead, telling her about the red dress I'd found at the mall, and how it had fit just right, and how I wanted it more than anything.

"Sounds pricey," Mom said.

So were the ballet lessons I'd wanted in kindergarten. Mom had said we couldn't afford them, but then she found a way. She always did, when it was something important.

"Please, Mom. The dress is perfect."

She rubbed her forehead. "I'll see what I can do."

That was Mom code for yes. I threw my arms around her and squeezed until she laughed and swatted me away.

The next morning, Leigh ignored me as we waited for the bus and then sat several rows away. Fine with me. She'd probably been reporting everything I said to Ava and her crew anyway. I yanked on a torn cuticle, furious I'd been tricked into thinking she was a friend. At least being mad at Leigh gave me something to focus on other than the meeting ahead.

My name was called over the intercom as soon as I walked in the front door. The secretary ushered me into the principal's office with a curt nod. Mrs. Zdinski sat behind her desk, which was even more dinged up than I remembered.

"Good morning, Felicity," she said, glancing up briefly from her computer and speaking in a formal voice. "Please have a seat."

I perched on the edge of one of the two chairs in front of her desk. Mrs. Zdinski kept typing like I wasn't even there.

Her short, dyed hair was arranged in grandmotherly curls so thin I could see right through them. There was a mole on her chin with a hair sticking out. My hands itched to reach out and pluck it, so I tucked them safely under my legs. The door opened, and Ms. Finley entered the room.

"Sorry I'm late," she said, adjusting her silky shirt. "There was an accident on Third and Bank that slowed things down this morning."

"Oh dear," Mrs. Zdinski said. "I hope everyone is okay."

Ms. Finley launched into a description of the accident as she settled into the chair next to me. One of my knees bounced as I struggled to control my jitters.

After they finished their small talk, Mrs. Zdinski turned to me. "You're a very lucky young lady. Ava wasn't injured yesterday. Still, her mother is quite upset and pushing for suspension."

I groaned. Of course Ava's mother was pushing for suspension.

"Ms. Finley convinced her that an apology will suffice, but I'm afraid she's still planning to report you to the pageant committee."

I sat up straight and jerked my hands free from under me. "What does the pageant have to do with any of this?"

Ms. Finley answered. "They have a behavior clause. Naturally they don't want a representative who will reflect poorly on their organization."

I'd always thought the phrase "brokenhearted" was a

metaphor, but my chest suddenly felt like my heart had actually been ripped in two. The pageant was my only hope. A flash of anger hit me. It wasn't fair that I was going to be disqualified for something that happened at school. Especially not something I hadn't even started. I narrowed my eyes. "Is Ava going to be disqualified, too?"

Mrs. Zdinski and Ms. Finley both raised their eyebrows. "Ava didn't hit anyone."

"So the pageant is okay with a bully representing them?"

"Ava insisted she didn't know why you attacked her," Mrs. Zdinski said, leaning forward. "If there's more to the story, now would be a good time to speak up."

I didn't think there was any chance I could save my spot in the pageant, but I had to try. "I know I shouldn't have hit her," I said after I finished explaining. "But I'm not the only one who acted like a jerk."

Mrs. Zdinski and Ms. Finley exchanged a look I didn't understand. Mrs. Zdinski clasped her hands and ran one thumb over the other like she wasn't quite sure what to do with this new information. "Thank you for sharing this with us," she finally said. "It's quite a different version of events than we were given yesterday."

I nearly snorted. Of course it was. It's not like little Ms. Perfect was going to admit she did anything wrong.

"I think perhaps, in light of this new information, I

might be able to convince Mrs. Benson to drop the entire matter," Ms. Finley said.

I looked up, filled with hope. "You mean I'll still be able to do the pageant?"

"I can't make any promises," she said. "But I suspect Mrs. Benson isn't going to want to risk Ava's participation. I'll see what I can do."

I blinked back the heat behind my eyes. "Thank you."

Ms. Finley nodded. "I'm disappointed in both of you. But I believe in second chances. Can I trust you won't let me down?"

I nodded vigorously. I'd win the crown and be the best pageant queen this state had ever seen.

I expected Ava's bullying to be worse than ever, and I heard plenty of whispers wherever I went, but Ava mostly acted like I didn't exist, which was a relief.

During lunch, I searched online for anything I could find about coyotes and badgers hunting together. I was sure I'd turn up empty-handed, but there were actually a few different videos documenting the same type of interaction I'd seen. I was disappointed that I hadn't made a new scientific discovery, but still, what I'd witnessed was pretty amazing. Apparently coyotes and badgers sometimes came together in something called a symbiotic relationship, where they worked with each other to make sure they both got their meals.

As I watched the videos, I noticed how comfortable the coyotes and badgers were with each other. I wondered if there was any more to their relationships—maybe they weren't only hunting partners, they were friends, too. Then again, I'd tried making friends with a different species, and look how well that had turned out.

On Saturday, Mom asked if I wanted to go with her to the Laundromat. She seemed to be getting better every day.

"Can we drop by the mall for my dress?" I asked hopefully. Ms. Finley had told me on Friday that Ava's mom had agreed not to report our fight as long as we stayed away from each other. The pageant was in three weeks, and I still had shoes to worry about.

"Not today," Mom said wearily.

"But Mom, the pageant—"

She held up a hand. "I haven't forgotten about the pageant."

Her tone made it clear the discussion was over.

I decided to stay home and rehearse my talent. I'd picked an old song called "Desperado." I didn't completely understand the lyrics, but I thought it was about an old cowboy, and I liked how his loneliness came through in the song. The music teacher at school had sent in the accompaniment I'd need for the pageant. Even though I didn't have a way to play the music, I spent part of the morning practicing.

I divided the rest of my time between studying the information Ms. Finley had given us about the interviews and perfecting my model walk, taking care to only do it when Larry was out working on the boat. If Mom hadn't told him about the pageant, I certainly wasn't going to spill the beans.

I tried hard to concentrate, but I kept checking out the window for Leigh. No signs of life came from her trailer all morning. She was probably off hanging out with Ava Benson. Not that I cared what she did, because I didn't. Not one bit.

I was eating a dry bologna sandwich—we'd run out of mayo a week earlier, and Mom said another jar wasn't in the budget for now—when the roar of Larry's truck told me Mom was home.

I went out to help her unload.

"Grab the laundry," she said, picking up a paper bag from the seat beside her.

"You went shopping?" I sniffed, hoping to pick up the scent of something delicious. Maybe she'd brought home a bag of chips. Or some bananas.

"Only to Twice as Good."

I frowned, lifting the laundry basket from the truck as I tried to figure out what she'd needed at the secondhand store. "What'd you get?"

"You'll see."

I lugged the basket inside and set it next to the table to

be sorted. Mom set her bag on the table and pulled out a pair of jeans with a big panel sewn in the front.

"What are those for?"

Mom grinned. "For when my stomach gets a little bigger."

She pulled out a pair of khakis that had the same kind of fabric.

"Why would your . . ."

I shook my head, hoping what I was thinking wasn't what she meant. I'd always wanted a little brother or sister, but not now. Not with him.

Mom smiled at me expectantly.

"Are you . . . ?"

"I'm pregnant!" She rubbed her belly like it was the best news in the world.

One time, she'd dated a guy who had taken us to a carnival that was passing through town. We'd ridden on a Tilt-A-Whirl, and when we got off it was like my brains had been scrambled. That's how I felt now. I didn't know whether to laugh or cry.

"What? When?"

Mom laughed. "It's a lot to take in, I know."

"You never had cancer, did you?"

"Cancer?" Mom rubbed her head. "Fud, where do you come up with these things?"

"You've been so sick, I thought—"

She sighed. "I suppose I should have told you sooner.

I wanted to get past the first trimester so you didn't get your hopes up."

I plopped down in a chair and picked at a tear in the vinyl seat. "Is it a boy or a girl?"

"We'll find out next spring."

"That's when the baby's due?"

"The best I can figure."

The best she could figure? I didn't know a lot about having babies, but when they were going to arrive seemed like an important detail. "Can't a doctor tell you?"

"I don't need a doctor," Mom said. "The baby will come when the baby comes."

She must not have noticed my doubt because she continued. "The timing is perfect. I'll have the baby here while Larry finishes up the boat."

The boat. A baby. The boat. A baby. I knotted my hands together, squeezing them tightly.

"Do you really think taking a baby on a boat is such a great idea?"

"I don't see why not."

"What if it falls overboard?"

"We won't have to worry about that until the baby starts crawling. And Larry said he could rig up some kind of harness."

Mom's eyes shone with excitement. Every cell in my body screamed that this was a bad idea, but I couldn't bring myself to wish the baby away now that it was here.

The thought of a brother or sister made my heart swell to ten times its normal size. I was going to take care of this baby and love it to the moon and back. That meant I had to change Mom's mind about their plan.

"What about the stinky diapers—where will they go?"

"We'll cross that bridge when we get to it."

I wanted to cross that bridge now. And the million other problems I could think of with taking a brand-new baby on a boat with Larry.

Mom's new macramé hung by the window. Most of the leaves dripping over the small planter nestled inside had turned from yellow to brown, telling me what I'd already known: the plant's days were numbered. "Maybe we should stay here, you know, until the baby is older."

"Maybe you should let me and Larry do the adulting." Mom's voice made it clear the conversation was over.

She reached her hand back in the bag. "Anyway, that's not the only surprise I have."

I was still trying to deal with the first surprise, but Mom pulled out a glittery piece of fabric and grinned. "Look what I found!"

She unfolded it to reveal a long, sequined evening gown. The whole thing was basically a straight line until it got above the chest, then it draped over the shoulder on one side exactly like something an eighty-year-old woman would wear.

"What's that?" I asked.

"Your pageant dress!" Mom beamed. "It'll look gorgeous on you."

The red dress I'd asked for had looked gorgeous on me. This dress was . . . I couldn't tell what color it was. I blinked several times, but it was no use. The world had faded to gray again.

I opened my mouth to tell Mom, then snapped it shut. She was so excited. And now that she was pregnant, she didn't need to be worrying about me.

She pulled something else from the bag. "I got these to go with it."

The shiny pumps were a little scuffed, and nothing like the shoes at the mall, but at least they were heels. And they'd hide my hairy toes.

"What do you think?" she asked, gesturing at the whole outfit.

"Yeah, it's—wow. Thanks, Mom." The dress was awful. Worse than awful. Worse, even, than the black dress I'd tried on in the store. But I couldn't tell her that—not when she'd tried so hard.

"Are you sure we can afford it?" I prayed she'd say it was too expensive and decide to return it.

"It was on the fifty-percent-off rack! There's a small tear in the back seam—"

She showed me a barely noticeable hole just below the zipper. "But that will be easy enough to fix. And Larry can do without his bacon next month."

"Maybe we should take it back. He won't be happy you spent his bacon budget."

"You let me worry about that." She pushed the dress into my hands. "Try it on."

I trudged toward the bathroom, where I peeled off my clothes and slid into the dress. When I turned to the cracked mirror above the sink, I did a double take. The dress was as ugly as sin, as Mom liked to say, and it made me look like an old lady.

I couldn't go onstage in this! My chest started to tighten, but I remembered the mountain lion attacking the coyote. The coyote didn't roll over and let the lion have her pups—even if winning had seemed like a long shot, she'd been determined to go out fighting.

And then there'd been the way the lady from the shoe shop had sauntered through the store. *Channel your inner Imani,* I told myself.

Stand up straight, core tight, shoulders back, I heard Ms. Finley say.

I lifted my chin, determined to make sure Larry's bacon budget didn't go to waste.

CHAPTER TWELVE

Leigh and I continued ignoring each other all the next week, which was fine by me. With a little brother or sister on the way, winning the pageant was more important than ever. As I approached the trailer Friday afternoon, angry sobs filled the air. I sprinted up the stairs.

Mom was slumped on the couch. Her hands covered her face as she cried.

"What's the matter?" I dropped my backpack and rushed to her side. "Is the baby okay?"

She wiped away her tears and rubbed the melon-sized lump that had replaced her normally flat stomach. "The baby's fine."

"What's wrong?" I was worried that Larry had hurt her again, but I didn't see any signs of bruising or swelling.

"Larry lost his job."

I collapsed next to her. "What happened?"

"Who knows?" She started crying again.

There were millions of ways this could go badly.

Since Larry owned this trailer, we wouldn't have to worry about rent, but where would we get groceries? And what if our electricity got shut off? That happened to Mom and me once, but luckily it had been in the spring when the days were getting longer and warmer so not having light or heat wasn't such a big deal. "What are we going to do?"

I waited for Mom to tell me that Larry would find another job. Or that she'd go back to work. That everything would be fine.

"Run and get me a Kleenex," she said, sniffing.

I brought back a wad of toilet paper and sat by her side as she blew her nose. A cluster of open beer cans littered the coffee table. "Where's Larry?"

Mom sniffed again. "Out looking for a new job."

"Drunk?"

"He had a few beers with lunch." She dabbed at her eyes. "I'm sure he'll be fine."

He'd had more than a few, if the empty cans were any indication. "Should he really be driving?"

"Who's going to stop him?" Another flood of tears cascaded down Mom's cheeks.

Hopefully the police. But that was a long shot—somehow, he always seemed to fly under the radar.

That night, the fighting was worse than ever. Larry was angry about the rice and tuna Mom had mixed together for dinner and accused her of tucking away his paychecks to spend money on crap for herself instead of buying meat and potatoes so he could eat properly. Then he claimed she'd run over a nail and caused the flat tire that made him late for work and gotten him fired. He even accused her of getting pregnant on purpose.

When the first coyote howled and the rest followed, I threw myself into sorting out their voices. I'd listened to all of the recordings over and over again and had finally made some progress. As far as I could tell, the pack that lived nearby had either five or six adults. Four of them had distinctive combinations of howls and barks. The last one or two were more difficult. It was either one super-vocal coyote with a wide range of sounds or it was two coyotes that sounded a lot alike. There were at least three pups, too.

Most nights, their sounds likely signaled other coyotes to keep out of their territory. Sometimes, there were also calls and responses that they probably used to keep in touch when they were out hunting. I listened hard, trying to identify the last one or two voices, but I didn't have any more luck that night than I did any other.

The next morning, I made my way into the kitchen, groggy and bleary-eyed. Mom forced a smile from the table. "How did you sleep?"

I couldn't believe she actually thought I could have slept through the racket, but I didn't want to upset her. "Fine. You?"

"Fine. Make yourself some toast."

I reached for the still-open bread bag. Only a butt remained. I hated butts, but I was too hungry to skip breakfast, so I popped it in the dinged-up toaster that only heated bread on one side. "Where's Larry?"

I pulled a plate from the cupboard. It was chipped on the edge, but I loved the delicate rose pattern. We'd had this one since I was little. I used to pull it out and pretend I was a princess having fancy tea.

"Working on the boat." Mom sat up straighter and rubbed her lower back. "There's been a change of plans."

My heart raced. Maybe she'd finally come to her senses. "What kind of a change?"

"The boat has been coming along faster than Larry expected. And now that he's not tied down by a job anymore, he'll be able to finish it up even more quickly."

"Sooo . . . ?" I didn't like where this was heading.

"So he thinks we'll be ready to take off in a few weeks. Isn't that great?" Mom's strained smile made it clear she was trying to convince herself as much as me.

"Uh . . ." I could think of about seven million reasons why it wasn't great, but I decided to start with the most important. "What about the baby?"

"What about it?" Mom rubbed her stomach.

"How are you going to have it on a boat?"

She let out a genuine laugh. "Fud, women have been having babies for thousands of years. Being on a boat isn't going to change that."

"But how are you going to get to the hospital?"

"Larry will deliver the baby." She bit into her toast. "We were planning a home birth anyway."

This was news to me, but Mom's eyes shone with excitement. Whatever her feelings about spending the winter on the boat, she was fully on board with this part of the plan.

My stomach roiled and twisted. I flushed, like I was suddenly spiking a fever. "He's not a doctor."

"He'll read some books. It's not that hard to catch a baby."

She said it matter-of-factly, like we were discussing whether to have Tater Tots for dinner.

The Laundromat had fancy front-load washers that let you watch your clothes spin. Now my thoughts did the same thing. Maybe she was right—maybe this wasn't a big deal. It's not like I was an expert on having babies.

But I was an expert on Larry, and I imagined him trying to catch a baby with one hand while holding a beer in the other. This whole thing was a terrible idea.

"This isn't my first rodeo," Mom said, trying to lighten the mood.

I pressed my lips together.

My toast popped up. I reached for it automatically and burned my fingertips. "Ouch!"

"Run your hand under cold water."

I turned on the faucet. Icy water rushed out, temporarily relieving the pain in my fingers. My eyes widened as I noticed my long, razor-sharp nails. I'd always bitten them to the quick.

I shut off the faucet. With everything going on, I must have broken the habit without even thinking about it. Once I trimmed them, my nails would be perfect for the pageant. As happy as this made me, it wasn't enough to wipe the scowl from my face.

Mom ran a frustrated hand through her hair. "I thought you'd be excited about this. You've always wanted to travel. This is your chance!"

I'd always wanted to travel with *Mom*. If something happened to her . . . The thought was too horrible to finish.

She had to know this was a bad idea. Like a wrestle-with-a-skunk kind of bad idea. But the look in her eyes was pleading. She wanted me to be excited. She *needed* me to be excited. I reviewed the calendar in my head. The pageant was in two weeks. It was going to be close, but with a little luck, we'd be gone before Larry finished the boat.

"Sounds great," I said.

Mom's smile showed her relief. I stabbed my knife

into the jar of crunchy peanut butter, feeling like more than my fingertips had been singed.

After breakfast, I trimmed my nails and then escaped into Mom's room, hoping to find an interview outfit for the pageant. She mostly wore yoga pants around the house, but a handful of dresses hung at the back of the closet, smelling of mint and perfume. I pressed my face into one. The last time Mom had worn it, we'd dressed up for no reason at all, and we'd turned on the radio and danced through the living room until we'd collapsed in a fit of giggles. I pulled the dress from the hanger, a fresh wave of determination chasing away my sudden sadness.

That dress was too small, and so were the next two. The fourth was a sweater dress that would have been perfect except moths had eaten holes through the fabric. The fifth she'd worn for Larry's birthday—it was too casual and way too worn. I pulled out the last dress. My ability to see color had faded in and out ever since that day on the bluff. Right now, it was out. Although this dress looked the same gray as the others, I was pretty sure it was brown. It belted around the waist and flared out from my hips. I almost didn't try it on, but there weren't any other options.

The dress was definitely out of style, but it fit me perfectly. I twirled in the mirror, admiring how the skirt floated around my legs. Then I dug in the closet some more, hoping Mom hadn't gotten rid of the brown platform boots I used to love wearing when I was a toddler.

I breathed a sigh of relief when I found them under an old quilt at the back of the closet. I was pretty sure I'd be the only one at the pageant wearing boots at my interview, but the pumps Mom had bought me would look terrible, and I couldn't very well show up in my sneakers.

I slipped the boots on. Leigh was going to love these.

Only Leigh and I weren't friends anymore.

I was doing the pageant for Mom and the baby, but I had to admit that all of this had been a whole lot more fun with Leigh. Everything had been more fun with her.

I thought you were my friend. Her words echoed in my head, making me cringe. Maybe she was right. Maybe I had jumped to conclusions. Maybe I'd taken my anger out on her when the person I'd really been angry at was myself.

I sat down on the edge of Mom's bed and traced a faded flower on the sheet. So much was out of my control right now. Trying to make things right with Leigh was one thing I could do. Or at least try.

I changed back into my regular clothes, grabbed my pageant heels, and marched straight to Leigh's trailer before I lost my courage. Two ghoulishly carved pumpkins greeted me at the top of their stairs. Click answered the door.

"Fud, it's so good to see you," she said, squeezing me in a friendly hug. Maybe Leigh hadn't told her we were fighting.

"Leigh," she yelled. "You have a visitor."

Leigh appeared in the doorway of her bedroom wearing leggings and a fuzzy sweater I thought was purple but couldn't tell for sure. When she saw me, she crossed her arms. "What are you doing here?"

"I'm going to leave you two to chat," Click said, disappearing into the back of the trailer.

Part of me wanted to snap back at Leigh. But I shouldn't have expected her to welcome me with open arms. I held up my heels. "I'm, uh, I'm practicing my pageant walk. I thought maybe we could do it together."

"What about Ava Benson?"

I bit my lip. "I shouldn't have said the things I did. And I definitely shouldn't have hit her. Please, can we be friends again?"

Leigh stood glowering at me like she really wanted to say no.

When canids like dogs, coyotes, and wolves show submission, they sometimes roll on their backs, exposing their soft underbellies. I imagined dropping to the floor and almost snickered. *Pull yourself together,* I lectured myself. *You have one chance to get this right.*

"I've really missed you," I said softly.

Tears filled Leigh's eyes as she rushed toward me. "I've missed you, too."

She gave me a big hug.

"So we're good?" I asked.

"We're good."

I breathed an enormous sigh of relief, surprised at how much lighter I felt.

When we pulled away, I pointed out the obvious. "Ava isn't going to be happy that we're friends again."

"Ava can go suck a sour lemon," Leigh said.

"What? I thought you liked her?"

"I told you, she has some good parts. But that doesn't mean I want to be her best friend or anything else. I can't be myself around her like I can with you."

That was exactly how I felt about Leigh. She didn't care that I never seemed to know what to do or say or that all my clothes were other people's leftovers.

"Come on," she said, pulling me toward her bedroom. "I've got to get my pageant shoes."

Leigh's bedroom hadn't changed a bit, except there was a small bowl of candy corn on her dresser. She pulled her heels out of the closet. Even though things were good between us again, I was still embarrassed by my feet, so I slipped on my heels when she wasn't looking.

"Are those the shoes you're wearing for the pageant?" she asked.

"Yep." I thrust up my chin defiantly.

"Oh, okay," she said. "That wasn't what I had in mind for you, but your dress is so spectacular it won't matter anyway."

"I got a different dress," I said, figuring I might as well rip off the Band-Aid right away.

Leigh flopped on her bed. "Tell me!"

I described the dress, trying to make it sound appealing.

"You're going vintage," Leigh said. "I like it."

If vintage meant old and cheap, then yes, I was going vintage. I studied her dresser, then I frowned. "Your photo is gone."

"It's in a drawer," Leigh said. "I couldn't stand looking at it every day."

She'd said that her life wasn't perfect. I'd been so focused on how lucky she was living with just her mom that I hadn't thought about how much it must have hurt when her dad left.

"I really am sorry for what I said."

"It's okay. I know you didn't mean it. And it's not exactly like I told you about my problems."

I hadn't been honest with her about my problems, either. The thought hovered in my mind like a pesky mosquito, but I slapped it away. She'd never be able to understand how much I longed for Larry to disappear from our lives.

Deep inside, I knew my silence was more than that.

It was like I was trapped at the top of the world's tallest cliff—there was no chance of inching my way down, of talking my way out of the danger. In order to escape, I'd have to leap. And I wasn't ready to do that yet. Not here, with her. Not until after I'd won the pageant.

A bright yellow giraffe with orange spots perched on her dresser. My color was back! I grabbed the giraffe and squeezed it to my chest like it might help me figure out what to say. "How long have your parents been divorced?"

"It was finalized right before we moved here, but they'd been separated for a couple of years."

"That must have been really hard."

"The hard part was how quickly he replaced me," Leigh said. Tears built up in her eyes. She clenched her jaw, trying to hold them back.

I wanted to tell her she hadn't been replaced, but I didn't know her dad. "He's a real idiot if he thinks some stupid baby can replace you."

Leigh laughed. "You're right. The baby can't do this."

She stood up and, even though she was in heels, bent into a bridge and then walked her legs over her head.

"Does he have something to do with why you gave up gymnastics?"

Leigh plopped down on the ground and picked at the carpet. "Sort of. I mean, Dad's a big reason we moved here—Mom couldn't stand living in the same city with him and his new wife. And my team—they were pretty much family. Mom said I could join the gym here, but—"

She shrugged. "It wouldn't be the same."

"Yeah, well, I'll bet your dumb sister never wins a beauty pageant," I said, trying again to lighten the mood.

Leigh's eyes lit up. "Dad said he'd come to the pageant."

"Is that why you're doing it?"

She continued picking at the carpet. "He almost never calls anymore. The only time I hear from him is when he sends pictures of the new baby. If I win, maybe he'll see that I'm worth something, too."

For a split second, I hoped Leigh would win, no matter how badly I needed the prize money.

"If you need a crown to show him that, then maybe *he's* the one who's not worth anything."

Leigh smiled sadly. "Thanks, Fud."

I smacked her over the head with the giraffe. "Sitting around talking isn't going to win either of us the crown. Let's get to work."

We spent the next half hour prancing around the trailer in our heels, practicing our model walks and turns. Finally, I sank down at the kitchen table.

Leigh threw a pack of gummies my way. "How are you going to do your hair for the pageant?"

I hadn't thought about it. "My usual ponytail, I guess?"

"You should wear it down."

I snorted. "I hear judges love frizzy curls."

"You just need some product," Leigh said. "I have something that might work."

I helped myself to a piece of jerky before I followed her into her bathroom. She rummaged under her sink and pulled out a bottle of something called Frizz-B-Gone.

"This should do the trick," she said. "Get your hair wet."

"That's a bad idea." Wetting my hair only made the frizz worse.

"Trust me."

I ran the water until it was warm and then stuck my head under the faucet. A bolt of panic shot through me as I flashed back to Larry forcing my head into the sink, but when I came up, Leigh had a fluffy towel waiting.

Once I squeezed the excess water from my hair, she directed me to massage in the coconut-scented cream. Then she sat me down on the toilet and plugged in her blow-dryer, which flared into a wide circle at the end of the barrel. She turned it on a low setting and held it away from my head while she scrunched my curls, but it still felt great since my wet hair had given me a chill.

She turned off the blow-dryer. "Fud, you're gorgeous!"

She positioned me in front of the mirror. *Wowza!* She'd transformed my hair from a dry, frizzy mess into perfect, silky curls that cascaded around my face.

She pushed the cream into my hand. "You have to use this every day."

I couldn't even imagine how much the cream cost. I tried to give it back. "I can't take this."

"You have to," Fud said. "My grandmother gave it to me, but I hardly ever use it. It's just going to waste."

I nearly hugged her. To Leigh, this was plain old hair cream. To me, it was friendship in a bottle.

CHAPTER THIRTEEN

Monday morning, I followed Leigh's instructions to tame my curls. Since I didn't have a diffuser, which Leigh had explained was the large circle on the end of her blow-dryer that prevented the hot air from hitting my hair directly, she said it would be better if I used my fingers to shape the ringlets and let them dry naturally. When I was done, I smiled at the stylish stranger in the mirror and imagined myself walking down the halls at school.

The smile fell off my face.

The last thing I needed was everyone staring. Besides, the kids at school would make fun of me for trying to be someone I was not.

I searched for a rubber band and swiped my hair back in a ponytail.

Regular old Fud stared at me from the mirror. *Better.*

Old Fud might not look as nice as the new-and-improved Fud, but at least she wouldn't draw any attention.

Leigh was already waiting for me outside her trailer.

"Why is your hair in a pony?" she asked. "Did you use the cream?"

"I used it," I mumbled.

"What happened? Didn't it look good?"

"It looked fine."

Leigh shook her head, confused.

"It's more comfortable like this."

"That's only because you're used to it. When we moved here, Mom told me change is almost always uncomfortable. But it's how we grow."

I didn't want to grow. I wanted to keep a low profile until after the pageant, and then I'd figure out what to do next.

"Besides, your hair is gorgeous down. And it's good practice. You'll feel more natural wearing it that way at the pageant."

I huffed as I stomped toward the bus stop, but she kept at it until I reached up and pulled the rubber band from my hair, freeing my curls.

Leigh squealed and rearranged them. "You look. So. Good."

I told myself I was worrying for nothing. No one paid any attention to me at school anyway, so no one would care if I had a new hairdo.

"Oh, and by the way," Leigh said, handing me the jean jacket she'd been carrying. "I've had this forever, and I never wear it, so Mom said I could give it to you."

"I'm not taking your jacket!"

"You have to," Leigh said. "It just sits in my closet. And it looked way better on you than it ever did on me."

I really wanted the jacket, but the thought of wearing hand-me-downs from my neighbor was humiliating. It was bad enough that I had to wear them from perfect strangers.

"Please, take it," Leigh said, pressing it toward me.

She wouldn't be giving it to me if she didn't know—or at least suspect—that I couldn't afford to buy my own. But I'd never seen her wear it, and it was dumb to let it sit in her closet.

"Thanks," I mumbled, slipping off my coat, which was a hand-me-down from Mom. I wished I had a mirror, but I could tell from Leigh's face that I looked good.

My shoulders pulled back and my chin lifted.

The bus rumbled up, and the driver opened the doors.

Mr. Frizzle gave me a friendly wink as I climbed the stairs. "Like the new 'do, kid."

We slid into our regular seats, and I glanced at my reflection in the window. A stranger stared at me. I smiled, and the stranger smiled back.

I'd been right—wearing my hair down was a mistake. As soon as I stepped off the bus, one of Ava Benson's friends pointed me out. Ava adjusted her AirPods, trying to pretend she didn't notice me, but fear flashed across her face as her gaze darted my way.

A thick lump of guilt lodged itself in my throat.

"Her mommy probably did her hair today," another of Ava's friends said.

"Knock it off," Leigh told them, hooking her arm around mine.

"Whatever." Ava grabbed her friends' elbows and practically shoved them toward the school.

Mom always joked that she had a super sniffer, but either the girls had really overdone it with their cosmetics or I was developing one, too. I nearly drowned in the scents of various shampoos, a dozen different makeup products, and perfume.

Ava's voice floated back to us. "She's such a freak."

The girls tittered.

I flinched.

"Don't let them get to you," Leigh said. "You look like a million bucks."

I searched my pocket for my rubber band. I appreciated that Leigh had finally started sticking up for me, but I didn't want to deal with this kind of attention all day.

My hand found only lint.

Great. Now I was stuck with my hair down.

"Hey, Fud, did you get a haircut?" someone yelled when I entered my homeroom.

At least a dozen kids turned my way.

"Has she always looked that good?" Tyler asked no one in particular. A few boys snickered.

I blushed. Tyler thought I looked good?

Who cares what he thinks?

I certainly didn't. But I reached up to make sure my curls were in place.

Ms. José-Fitzgerald entered the room, heels clicking. After the morning announcements, she started dividing us into small groups to review for an upcoming test.

Tyler's hand shot in the air. "Can I be in Fud's group?"

Wait, what? Confusion tumbled inside me, making my stomach feel like the dryer at the Laundromat.

Ms. José-Fitzgerald shrugged. "I don't see why not."

Tyler pumped his fist in the air. "Yes."

Ms. José-Fitzgerald assigned Lamonte and a girl I hardly knew to our group, too. We pulled our desks together. I ended up right next to Tyler. He smelled fresh, like laundry soap and a hint of fruit. He ran a hand through his thick hair. I shifted on my seat, telling myself it was no big deal to be sitting next to the coolest boy in school but painfully aware of his every move.

Lamonte sat directly opposite me, scowling. I wondered what had gotten into him.

"I have to get an A on this test," the girl—Sophie— said. "Or else I'm grounded."

She immediately started asking practice questions. "What is a cell?"

"That's easy," I said. "The building block of living organisms."

"What are the two types?"

"Prokaryotic and eukaryotic," Lamonte and I said at exactly the same time. Our eyes met, and a shiver ran through me. His black skin was smooth. A small raised scar stood out on his cheek. That was new. I wanted to ask him about it, but I pressed my lips shut and dropped my gaze.

What is happening right now?

"I like the new hair," Tyler said.

"Thanks." I ducked my head, flustered.

"We should study together sometime."

Study together? Suddenly whatever was happening in my stomach felt more like food poisoning. Getting a compliment from Tyler was one thing. That didn't mean I wanted to go on a date.

"What's the next question?" Lamonte asked gruffly.

"Name the parts of a cell," Sophie said.

"Nucleus, cytoplasm, wall, and membrane," Lamonte said.

As she continued asking questions, Tyler bumped his knee up against mine. I moved my knee away, but he found it again. Then he started high-fiving me after almost every question, and pretty soon I had the feeling he was touching me every chance he got.

The smell of whatever hair product he used filled my

nose. It was supposed to be a fresh citrus scent, but it smelled like cleaning products. I turned my head, searching for fresh air.

Tyler's knee bumped mine again. My fist tightened. I was tempted to pop him in the nose. But I remembered Ava's scared eyes. And how happy Larry had been after I'd pummeled her.

"I have to go to the bathroom." I jumped up from my seat.

"Need an escort?" Tyler asked with a grin I suspected he thought was flirty but made me want to vomit.

"I think she can handle it on her own," Lamonte said.

I threw him a grateful glance as I grabbed a hall pass.

Fake yellow light glowed in the bathroom, which smelled of bleach. I splashed cold water on my face, trying to calm myself down.

A few weeks ago, I might have been thrilled if a boy—even one as obnoxious as Tyler—had paid me this kind of attention. But I hated that all this was because I'd changed how I looked on the outside.

I dawdled, washing and rewashing my hands.

Being pretty was apparently a kind of superpower—it attracted people like magnets.

That was good news when it came to getting into pageants—not so great when it drew a target on your back. Especially not when someone like Tyler was holding the rifle.

CHAPTER FOURTEEN

The next day, I pulled my hair into a ponytail without using any of Leigh's product. I left the jean jacket at home, too. When she asked why, I made up an excuse about how I'd woken up late. In homeroom, Tyler greeted me with his fingers pointed into guns and a smooth "What's up?"

It was like now that he'd noticed me, he couldn't stand that I wasn't falling all over him. I was on guard all week, fending off his unwanted attention in class, in the hallways—even at lunch. Besides his fruity smell, the school reeked of sweat, a million beauty products, and the pine-scented soap they used to scrub the floors. The combination made sitting near him—and school in general—almost unbearable.

At the same time, Larry had been working around the clock to finish up the boat. The cabin was done, and he said we could take off as soon as he got his hands on a motor. I wasn't much for prayers, but each night I begged God—or anyone else who was listening—to make sure he didn't find one before the pageant.

With the big day only a week out, Leigh and I planned to do a full run-through with our makeup and clothes Saturday morning. I was so nervous the night before that I could hardly sleep. My dresses were hopelessly dated. And singing to myself was one thing, but I wasn't used to an audience. If I was this nervous with Leigh, how was I going to hold up during the actual pageant?

I was still in bed when Larry yelled that he couldn't find the nail clippers. I leaped from my raft and swiped the clippers from my nightstand, cursing myself for not returning them to the bathroom when I was done using them the night before.

"Here they are," I said, tapping on the bathroom door. He opened it wearing nothing but a ratty bath towel wrapped around his waist. Steam poured into the hallway. I looked away and tried not to inhale the spicy scent of his cheap aftershave as he launched into a tirade about how this was his home and when he wanted something, he expected it to be in the right place.

Mom's head poked into the hallway from the kitchen. "It's almost breakfast."

Larry slammed the door in my face. I breathed a sigh of relief.

I was already dressed and sitting at the table when he entered the kitchen. His wet hair was slicked back, and he was wearing his normal work jeans and a T-shirt that said "real men sweat."

Mom jumped up from the table and started spooning him a bowl of oatmeal. "We're out of honey, but there's still a bit of peanut butter left."

He sniffed the air. "Where's the bacon?"

Mom's gaze darted my way as she used a knife to scrape the last of the peanut butter out of the jar. "It wasn't in the budget this month."

Oh, no. My heart thumped.

"It wasn't in the budget?" Larry's voice pulsed with anger.

"I know you're saving everything for the boat, and Fud needed a few extra things for school, and—"

I swallowed a groan. Why did she have to bring me into it?

A vein throbbed in Larry's temple. He spoke to Mom, but his furious gaze settled on me. "So let me get this straight. I'm out there in the cold, working my tail off to make the boat comfortable for you and our little peach—"

Little peach?

"—and instead of feeding me properly, you used our money—*my* money—to buy school supplies for this spoiled little brat?"

Anger coursed through me. I quivered, longing to throw myself at him, to wrestle him to the ground.

Mom started to protest. "No, that's not what I—"

Larry yanked me to my feet. "Let's go."

"Where?"

"I need some help with the boat. It's about time you started earning your keep around here."

I stumbled to keep up as he dragged me across the room, squeezing my arm tightly.

I resisted the urge to yelp. The wild feeling that I'd had when I'd attacked Ava pulsed inside me. It was all I could do not to bite his hand. Larry would kill me if I fought back, but the temptation was so strong it actually scared me. It was like there was an animal inside me, snarling and pawing at my insides, determined to get out.

Mom spoke up. "It's cold out there. At least let her put on a jacket."

He released my arm long enough for me to reach for my coat. As I tugged it on, Mom shot me a glance that seemed to be part warning (do what he says) and part regret (sorry this is happening).

Heat blazed inside me, and I shot back my own glance. It was part anger (how can you let this happen?) and part desperation (please, help me).

Mom tucked her head as Larry wrenched open the door. An icy wind carried the first few snowflakes of the season. His fist squeezed my arm like a handcuff. Again, I fought the urge to bite him. I peeked back to see Mom's gaze fixed on the floor.

Larry pushed me outside, causing me to stumble. He wanted to be treated like an alpha, but alphas had to earn the respect of their pack. The caged animal inside me broke free. I wrenched my arm from his grip, throwing myself off balance. The world tilted. I tumbled down the stairs, landing in a crumpled ball at the bottom.

It wasn't until I moved my arm and saw my left hand dangling at a gruesome ninety-degree angle that a blinding pain shot through me, a fireball radiating from my wrist.

"Ouch," I yelped. Moments before, I'd been strong and fierce. Now, I was nothing more than a cowering pup.

"Get your butt up," Larry growled.

I started to climb to my knees but ended up hunched over, clutching my arm to my chest as I sobbed.

"What's going on out here?" Mom poked her head out the door.

Larry bent over me, pushing up my coat and examining my wrist with surprisingly gentle touches. He let out a long string of curse words that might have made my ears bleed if I wasn't already used to them.

"Grab the keys and some ice," he told Mom, whipping out a pocket knife and cutting the sleeve off my coat.

Minutes later, we sped down the highway in a truck that for some reason smelled like roast beef. I was squished between Mom and Larry. Tears streamed down my cheeks as Mom pressed a sandwich bag full of ice to my wrist.

"Knock off the crying," Larry barked.

"She's hurting," Mom said, grabbing my good hand.

"She's no baby. She needs to toughen up."

A small sob escaped my mouth.

Larry's hands gripped the wheel, causing his knuckles to turn white. "Do you know how many bones I've broken in the ring?"

He didn't wait for me to answer. "More than I can count. And do you know how many times I cried about them? None. So knock it off."

He reached for the radio and fiddled with the knobs, cursing as he searched for something other than static. The only station that came in clearly was country music, which Mom and I liked okay, but Larry wasn't a big fan. A song by Martina something-or-other came on. It was a sad song about a girl hiding her bruises by being as hard as stone.

When it got to the part about her turning into an angel and flying up to a place where she's loved, Larry muttered something about it being too much to ask to get a decent song on the radio these days and shut it off. Mom put her arm around me. I leaned into her shoulder, desperately trying to hold back my tears.

The ride to town had never felt longer. Or bumpier. An explosion of pain shot through my arm with each hole in the road. And the hospital was all the way over on the other side of town. Larry dropped Mom and me at the emergency room and went to park the truck. A woman wearing green scrubs hurried us into a small room that held an exam table and a computer and reeked of Band-Aids and cleaning products. She helped me settle on the table and gave Mom a clipboard with some paperwork.

"The doctor is on call," she said. "He should be here shortly."

The door closed and didn't open again until Larry walked in. By now, I was wracked with chills and shaking uncontrollably.

He ranted about the hospital's terrible care—something about cutting costs to make a buck—before poking his head back into the hallway. "Hey, we need some help over here."

Another lady dressed in scrubs responded to his call. Her dark hair was pulled back, and she had a beauty mark on her brown cheek.

"She needs blankets," Larry said harshly. "And something for the pain."

"Please," Mom added, trying to soften Larry's demands.

He glowered at her. Mom's gaze dropped to the floor.

"I'll see what I can do." The nurse's tone was polite, but I had a feeling she didn't care much for Larry. She returned before long with two heated blankets, which she wrapped around my shoulders. "There you go, sweetheart," she said gently.

I moaned as the warmth enveloped me, easing my discomfort ever so slightly.

"What about the pain?" Larry asked.

"I can't give her anything without a doctor's order." Her cold voice had returned.

I kept my eyes focused on the wallpaper, which featured a parade of animals walking one after the other like they were lining up for the ark but had forgotten their partners. I suspected the colors were bright, but my eyes weren't working right again.

"Well, I'm her parent, and I say you'd better get her something right now," Larry said.

This didn't seem like a good time to remind him that he *wasn't* my parent.

"I'm sorry, sir, that's not possible."

He towered over her. "You're telling me you can't even give the kid an aspirin? What kind of crap place is this? I knew you were all quacks."

"If you don't calm down, I'm going to have to call security. The doctor should be here shortly."

"Yeah, well, he'd better be."

The sharks were swimming around in my stomach again, but instead of swallowing me whole, I wished they'd swallow Larry. Or at least shut him up.

He sank down in the chair. Mom set aside the clipboard and stood beside me, clutching my good hand. I lost track of time as I fought against the tears that refused to leave me alone, but it felt like an hour had passed before Larry opened the door again and hollered. "Did you forget about us?"

The same nurse that brought me the blankets responded.

"I'm sorry, sir, but there's been an accident that requires the doctor's immediate attention. He'll get to you as soon as he can."

Larry towered over her again, his face flushed. "This girl needs help now."

"I need you to calm down, sir. We're doing the best we can."

"Do your job and you won't have to worry about me calming down."

He was flat-out yelling at the nurse now. She picked up the phone and called for security.

"Don't bother." Larry pushed the blankets off my shoulders and scooped me off the table.

I yelped.

"I can't let you leave," the nurse said. "This child needs medical attention."

"I'd like to see you stop me."

I didn't want to leave, and I definitely didn't want to give up the blankets I'd been wrapped in, but we were already out the door.

The nurse hurried after us. "Sir, the next nearest hospital is at least an hour from here."

Larry paused to let the sliding doors open. "That'll save us time if they actually treat their patients," he called over his shoulder.

I whimpered as we stepped out into the cold.

The nurse continued trying to reason with Larry. "You'll have to sign a waiver acknowledging that you're leaving against medical advi—"

The doors shut behind us. Larry's angry strides made the pain in my throbbing wrist nearly unbearable. I focused every ounce of energy on controlling my tears as he deposited me in the cab and circled the truck to sit behind the wheel.

"What now?" Mom climbed in beside me and slammed her door.

"Now we find a real hospital," Larry said, turning the key. The truck roared to life.

The woman who had originally checked me in came running toward the truck. "Wait," she yelled.

Mom rolled down her window, letting in a blast of cold air. "What is it?"

The woman shoved some papers at Mom. "You didn't fill out your paperwork. We need a signature on the AMA, your insurance information, and an address where we can send the bill."

"What for?" Mom crumpled the papers into a ball and tossed it back at the lady. It bounced off her chest and fell to the ground. "You didn't do anything."

Larry shifted the truck into drive and we peeled out of the parking lot.

The hour-long ride to the next hospital lasted a thousand years. When we got there, they hurried me into an exam room that didn't have any childish wallpaper but smelled of the same cleaning products as the first hospital. The doctor arrived only moments later. He was a plump Indian man with kindly eyes and a slight accent. "How did this happen?"

"She fell down the stairs," Larry said.

"I'd like to hear from her," the doctor said. He consulted my chart. "Felicity, how did you fall down the stairs?"

Larry crossed his arms over his chest, flexing his muscles. Mom's head angled down, her long hair hiding her face.

It had all been so quick. One minute, I was at the top of the stairs. The next, I was at the bottom. "I tripped."

"By accident?"

"Of course it was by accident," Larry said. "What are you getting at?"

"Sir," the doctor said firmly. "I'm going to need you to wait outside."

Anger radiated off Larry in waves, filling the room with his silent fury.

I tensed.

The doctor held Larry's gaze and motioned toward the

door. "You can make yourself comfortable in the lobby."

A muscle in Larry's jaw pulsed as he shifted from one foot to another. His fist opened and shut like he was aching to teach the guy a lesson.

My lungs forgot how to pull in air.

"Freakin' quack," Larry muttered, storming from the room.

I gaped. But before I had the time to figure out what kind of magic the doctor had just pulled, he turned to Mom.

"Ma'am." He motioned for her to follow Larry out.

I didn't see why he had to kick her out, too, but I wasn't going to argue with a guy who could out-stare Larry.

Mom searched my face. A worried wrinkle creased her brow. I gave her a weak smile, doing my best to reassure her that I'd be fine. For a second, I thought she was going to insist on staying, but she gave my good hand a quick squeeze and followed Larry to the lobby.

As the doctor closed the door, I thought a flash of relief crossed his face. But when he turned to me, it was gone. "This is a safe space," he said briskly. "You can speak freely."

I almost snorted. He might have cowed Larry into leaving the room, but at some point, I'd have to face him again.

The doctor was still talking. "I'm going to ask you a

very important question, and I want you to think carefully about your answer."

I nodded, but he didn't have to worry. After the scene Larry had made, I wasn't going to give him any trouble.

"Was your fall an accident?"

"I think so?"

"You don't know for sure?"

I'd been the one to jerk my arm away from Larry. "We were leaving the trailer, and I lost my balance going down the stairs. I've always been clumsy." I added the last bit for good measure.

"No one pushed you?" the doctor asked, more gently this time.

I heard Larry's fists hitting his punching bag. *Thwap. Thwap. Thwap.* It wasn't fair to blame him for something I'd started. "Like I said, I'm clumsy."

The doctor narrowed his eyes and studied me for a moment before announcing he'd have to set my wrist before putting on a cast.

A vague sense of disappointment bubbled inside me. He should have asked me if I ever worried about being hurt. Or if anyone in my house had ever been hurt. But I probably wouldn't have said anything anyway. As the doctor worked on my wrist, I gritted my teeth and pretended I was made of stone.

CHAPTER FIFTEEN

Larry was surprisingly nice all day Sunday. He even excused me from doing the dishes. Monday morning he poked his head out from the boat.

"Make sure you keep that sling on," he said gruffly.

I nodded without meeting his eyes.

Leigh rushed outside as I neared her trailer. She wrapped her arms around me, bumping my cast. I groaned as a small bolt of pain shot through my wrist.

"Sorry," she said, pulling back and adjusting her sparkling headband. "I'm so happy to see you. I was worried when you didn't come over on Saturday. I tried to visit yesterday, but your mom said you were sleeping. I'm really sorry you're hurt."

She finally took a breath. "What happened?"

I adjusted my backpack with my good arm.

"Do you need me to carry that?" she asked.

"I'm good. I fell down the stairs."

"Seriously?" she laughed. "You've got to make up a better story than that. Tell everyone that you tripped running from aliens. No, tell them you were injured *fighting* aliens! But wait—" She spun toward me. "Does that mean you can't do the pageant?"

"What? No! I'm still doing the pageant." Worry coiled itself in my stomach like a venomous snake. "I mean I think I'm still doing it. If they'll let me."

Leigh eyed my cast. "Well, they'll definitely remember you."

I hadn't thought about the pageant when the doctor asked what color cast I preferred. Now I wanted to slap my forehead. I should have asked for something neutral. But no, I had to go and ask for turquoise. Still, my broken arm was only temporary. The judges had to be able to see that.

Once we were settled on the bus, Leigh used a marker to sign her name, adding BFF and a heart, which made me both happy and sad. For a second, I considered telling her everything—about the boat, about Larry, about his plans. But I couldn't.

Larry had already hurt Mom. I couldn't even begin to imagine what he'd do to her—to us—if he found out I was telling people what it was like to live with him.

The skin under my cast itched. I squirmed, trying to find some relief.

"Are you okay?" Leigh asked.

I said I was fine, but there wasn't a single bone in my body that meant it.

* * *

When I got off the bus, everyone wanted to sign my cast. Tyler drew a Halloween pumpkin and scrawled "T-man" and then flung an arm over my shoulder, making me squirm to get away. Lamonte asked if he could sign, too. He smelled so good I was tempted to lick his cheek while he was doing it.

After his signature, he drew a picture of a small dog.

"Thanks," I said, smiling shyly. "It's really cute."

He grinned. "It's my dog, Chester. He always makes me feel better, so I thought maybe he could do the same for you. By the way, I've been meaning to tell you good luck in the pageant this weekend. I'm rooting for you."

"What was that all about?" Leigh asked after he walked away.

"What?" I asked, trying to act innocent.

"Come on," she said. "That was some next-level flirting."

"It was not." I snuck a glance around to see if anyone had overheard. "He doesn't even like me."

But my heart thumped a hopeful beat in my chest, and I realized that Leigh might be right. Lamonte had always been nice to me, but this did seem like something . . . more. And there was a small, itty-bitty part of me that wanted to admit that I liked him, too.

Get real, I reminded myself. Boys like Lamonte didn't go for girls like me.

* * *

Each day after school, I half expected to find Mom packing our bags. But Larry's progress on the boat seemed to have stalled. I wasn't about to complain. Instead, I threw myself into practicing with Leigh for my interview. I showed her my dress. A brief flicker in her eyes confirmed it was every bit as bad as I thought, but she assured me that I could win the pageant wearing a paper bag.

My hope grew, along with my guilt. I opened my mouth a million times to tell Leigh that one way or another, I'd be leaving soon. Each time, I closed it again without saying anything.

Explaining I might be stuck on the boat with Larry would make it too real. And admitting that my only chance of escaping that fate rested on winning the pageant felt too big to say out loud. I vowed to tell her everything the moment I won. I forced my fear into a trapdoor somewhere deep in my chest and focused on the hope that I carried around like a delicate bubble ready to burst with the slightest touch.

On Friday afternoon, Larry was in his chair drinking beer and raging about why no one would cut him a break.

I spent the rest of the afternoon in my room, hoping to avoid the worst of his anger. Before dinner, his truck roared away from the trailer, and I breathed a sigh of relief.

By bedtime, he still hadn't returned. I tossed restlessly, listening for the truck and preparing myself for the fight that would undoubtedly come along with it.

A single coyote howled outside. I waited for the pack to respond, but there was only silence. The coyote howled again and then let out several barks. I recognized the voice, but the cadence was different tonight. Harsher. Angrier than usual. *Keep moving. This is my territory*, it seemed to say.

The pups yipped, their vocalizations ringing out from a different direction. But tonight their voices weren't bright and strong. They were full of sadness and longing. *Come back, Mama. We miss you.*

I pictured a group of pups waiting in a den for a mother that hadn't returned. They were probably cold. And hungry. And maybe even scared. I snorted, trying to convince myself I was reading things into the vocalizations that weren't really there.

Larry's truck rumbled into the driveway. The trailer door slammed. I waited for the yelling to start, but there was only the creak of his bedroom door shutting and then silence.

Still, I couldn't relax. Not when everything was riding on the next several hours. My brain raced out of control as I reviewed the information I'd memorized for the interview and the words to "Desperado" again and again. Eventually, I fell into a hazy dream about a coyote standing upright in a boxing ring with gloves on, punching someone whose face I couldn't see.

Despite my terrible night's sleep, I was up early the next morning. I planned to make a few trips to get everything I needed over to Leigh's house on account of only being able to use one arm, but she knocked before I'd even left my room. Mom called for me, and I entered the kitchen to find it cluttered with moving boxes.

"What's all this?" Leigh asked, the frown on her face mirroring my own.

"Larry got a motor for the boat," Mom said. "We're leaving tomorrow."

I stood frozen to the floor. Leigh wasn't supposed to find out like this.

"Leaving to where?" she asked at the same time I said, "Got a motor how?"

"Didn't Fud tell you?" Mom answered Leigh's question first. "We're going to live on the boat."

She turned to me. "He sold the trailer. There's enough for the motor and cash to keep us afloat through the winter."

Mom's eyes sparkled. She was actually excited about this new development.

My gaze met Leigh's. Tears welled in her eyes as she gripped a fuzzy red scarf wrapped around her neck. "You're moving?"

I blinked. Usually when the color went out in my

world, it was gradual. This time, it was a sudden switch. One second, her scarf was red; the next, it was gray. It was a good thing the pageant was today, because I definitely needed to see a doctor. "I was going to tell you right after the pageant."

"I'm happy we'll have a chance to get used to the boat before the baby comes." Mom rubbed her stomach.

Leigh forced a fake smile onto her face. "Sounds like a real adventure."

"Leigh," I said, wanting to make things right.

"Where are your outfits?" she asked. "We'd better get going."

I dropped my bag on the floor and disappeared down the hallway.

When I returned to the kitchen with my dresses, Leigh was already halfway out the door, my bag slung over her shoulder. I followed her outside in silence. It was like the glaciers that used to cover this part of the state had come back, and there was an entire mountain of ice between us.

I opened my mouth to explain, but Leigh held up her hand. "I don't want to talk about it right now," she said. "I have a pageant to win."

I swallowed hard. I had a pageant to win, too.

Click dropped us off in front of the convention center— an enormous glass building on the edge of town that I'd never seen until today. Leigh's outfits were in garment bags while mine were only on hangers. We waited on the sidewalk with our dresses folded over our arms and our bags at our feet while Click parked the car. Leigh turned away, acting like I wasn't even there.

I couldn't blame her—I'd be angry at me, too, if I were her. I studied her outfit, hoping she'd turn around and make eye contact, giving me some sort of opening to apologize. She was wearing leggings and a sweater in a color I couldn't recognize, but most of the girls arriving were dressed in sweats like me. Some of them were wearing winter coats. I hadn't gotten a new one since Larry sliced the arm off my old one, but the icy wind made me wish I'd thought to grab the jean jacket I'd been wearing in its place.

One girl caught my attention with a knitted headband that had wolf ears sticking up out of it. Another girl wore fluffy earmuffs, reminding me of the little rich girl in a book I'd read in school. Both girls were gorgeous. My stomach did one of Leigh's fancy flips.

Click arrived with a duffel bag slung over her shoulder, and we hurried inside. The lobby was cavernous. The sound of rolling bags and excited voices echoed off the shiny walls. A slight woman with a round face and dark skin greeted us with a clipboard. She was perfectly polished, from her glossy hair to her manicured nails.

"I'm Ms. Kora," she said. "And you are . . . ?"

Leigh and I gave her our names.

She eyed my cast. "Will you be participating in your . . . condition?"

I adjusted my sling.

"She will," Click said firmly.

Ms. Kora pursed her lips, and I held my breath until she checked our names off her list. As we passed Ballroom A, I caught a glimpse of rows and rows of chairs set up in front of a stage. Soon, those chairs would be filled with people. And judges. My heart thundered in my chest. *Don't freak out*, I told myself.

But it was hard not to, especially when we entered Ballroom B. Fancy wall panels and glittering chandeliers made it feel more like a palace than a conference center. Temporary stations surrounded by velvet curtains that I guessed were red had been set up in rows. The enormous room teemed with people. The air smelled of every kind of perfume and makeup on the planet, making my nose sting.

Ms. Kora explained that we'd all been assigned stations based on our last names.

That meant Leigh and I would be nowhere near each other. This wasn't how I'd expected the pageant to go. Leigh's confidence was infectious. Now, I was on my own. Worse, I was pretty sure I'd lost her friendship for good.

She made a point of ignoring me when we dropped her off at her station, which had a small makeup table, full-length mirror, and a clothing rack. Click came along

to make sure I got settled at my station, which was identical. "Here," she said, handing me a small brown paper
bag before she left. "I packed a bit of lunch in case you
forgot."

"Thank you," I said. Food hadn't even occurred to me.

Most of the day was spent standing around waiting
until Ms. Kora or one of her assistants shepherded us
onto the stage. I passed the time by fuming about the
boat, debating whether or not to apologize to Leigh, and
trying not to throw up at the thought of crossing the
stage in my heels.

We practiced where to walk, where to stop, and where
to exit. When I messed up my cue and bumped into the
girl in front of me, the other girls snickered.

"Stay away from her," Ava warned everyone.
"Seriously, she actually tried to bite me once."

A few girls gasped.

I hadn't realized Ava had known I'd been about to
bite her when Ms. Finley pulled me off. I fought the heat
flooding my face. *Don't let her get under your skin,* I
reminded myself.

The ballrooms didn't have any windows, so I couldn't
tell what time of day it was, but we were finally sent back
to our stations with strict instructions to stay quiet as
we prepared for the opening announcements. Apparently
the audience would be able to hear our chatter through
the thin ballroom walls.

I suspected most girls would have special outfits to demonstrate their talents. Since I didn't have that option, I made sure there weren't any gaps in the curtains around my station and pulled on the dress I'd borrowed from Mom. After belting it around my waist and tugging on her platform boots, which was no easy feat with one hand, I put my cast back in its sling and sat down at the makeup table to begin working on my hair.

I'd brought along the cream Leigh had given me, along with a squirt bottle filled with water that Mom kept under our sink to spritz her plants. As my curls took shape, my confidence grew. I'd put a lot of work into winning this pageant. If I'd been pretty enough to catch Tyler's attention, then I could catch the judges', too.

"Knock-knock." Click entered carrying a makeup palette. "Leigh said she's too nervous to do your makeup. But I've got you covered."

My face must have given away my hurt.

"Give her time," Click said softly. "She'll come around."

Hopefully she would "come around" before my departure.

Click worked in silence for several minutes. I was worried that she'd comment on the bushy eyebrows I'd been too nervous to try to shape, but she didn't mention them. Finally, she spun me around to face the mirror. I gasped.

My makeup was so dark and heavy I hardly recognized myself. There wouldn't be enough toothbrushes in the world if Larry caught me looking like this.

"Trust me," Click said. "The stage lights will wash you out."

"Thank you." I fought to keep the wobble from my voice. "I wouldn't have been able to do any of this without you."

It was more than the makeup. If it wasn't for her photos, I wouldn't be here. Not to mention the ride, the food—all of it.

Click laughed. "Save it for your acceptance speech." She rested a hand on my shoulder. "I have to go take my seat. Whatever happens this evening, I'm proud of you."

She gave me a hug, and I must have clung to her a little longer than she expected, because she finally laughed again and disentangled herself. She set her hand on my chin. "You've got this."

I hoped she was right.

CHAPTER SIXTEEN

We all lined up in a preassigned order. Ava Benson stood two girls in front of me, dressed in a miniskirt, frilly blouse, and cowgirl boots. Scowling, I turned my attention to the line behind me, where I located Leigh. Our gazes met briefly before she glanced away without acknowledging me. Her powder-blue leotard (one of the only shades I could still make out), matching eyeshadow, and sleek bun made her look like a professional gymnast. I wanted to wish her luck, but Mom always said it wasn't a good idea to poke the bear.

The MC, a local radio guy with a booming voice, welcomed the crowd and kicked things off by thanking the coal mine and introducing the seven former queens who were able to attend tonight's event. My ears perked up when I heard Ms. Finley's name. She glided across the stage in a flashy sequined dress. Although she was several sizes larger than the other former queens, she outshone them all with a smile so bright it could probably be seen from the moon. She must have felt me looking, because she met my gaze, then quickly glanced away.

Heat rushed to my face. We hadn't talked since the incident with Ava. This pageant was my chance to show her I was something more than a girl who went around attacking people.

After the former queens exited the stage, the MC announced the first contestant for the talent portion of the pageant, a petite girl dressed in a velvet sweatsuit and carrying a jumping rope.

She flashed a happy grin and launched into her routine. After that, one girl played the flute, one did a comedy routine, and one spun a million Hula-Hoops on all different parts of her body. My throat felt like I'd swallowed steel wool. Hopefully, my voice would hold up long enough for me to make it through a song.

Then the MC announced that Ava was up, and that she'd be singing a song she'd written herself. I froze. I should have known I wouldn't be the only person singing, but why did it have to be Ava sharing my talent? And how could I hope to compete against a singer-songwriter?

She strutted onstage. As soon as she opened her mouth, I realized I was in trouble. Big trouble. When Leigh had asked if I could sing, I'd said yes. Everyone could sing! And it wasn't like I hadn't practiced.

Ava's silky voice curled through the air. I'd seriously misjudged what they were expecting for talent. They were looking for *real* talent. Professional-level talent.

My singing was fine, but it wasn't *that*.

My gaze darted around the wings of the stage as I contemplated bolting. A long banquet table rested nearby, piled with snack foods in case we were hungry. A shiny metal bowl overflowed with fuzzy peaches, reminding me of how Larry had called the baby his "little peach."

I couldn't run away. Mom and the baby were counting on me, even if they didn't know it.

Ava finished singing. The next two girls took their turns, but I was too busy trying not to freak out to pay attention. My heart pounded louder than a charging herd of bison. Or maybe I was having a heart attack. Too soon, the MC called my name.

Ms. Kora nudged me.

I stepped out from behind the curtains. The bright lights made it impossible to see anybody in the audience beyond the five judges in the front row. Three of them were scribbling notes on the papers in front of them. The other two watched me cross the stage, their eyes wide. The heavy thump of my boots echoed with every step.

I stopped in front of the microphone, hoping the judges couldn't see the sweat gathering under my arms. The music started, but my mouth refused to open. The audience tittered. The judges scowled.

"Would you like to start over?" the MC asked, motioning for the music to stop.

Starting over wouldn't do any good. I had to come up with a new talent.

I leaned into the microphone and cleared my throat, hoping to buy some time. "I'm sorry—"

SCREEEEEEEE!

Everyone in the audience cringed. I tried again. "I'm sorry—"

SCREEEEEEEEE!

The MC, who was standing off to the side of the stage in a tuxedo, motioned for me to lean away from the microphone. I did, and this time it broadcast my voice clearly. I apologized for the change in plans and continued scrambling for a new idea. I couldn't Hula-Hoop or do gymnastics or tell funny jokes. Silence filled the auditorium. I had an urge to lift my chin and let out a long, mournful howl. That gave me an idea.

"You've already heard some beautiful singing today, so I'm going to share another talent with you. I'm going to teach you how to communicate with coyotes."

The crowd tittered again. Maybe it was a dumb idea, but it was the best I had. "*Coyote* comes from the Aztec word for 'trickster,'" I said. "But their scientific name basically means 'barking dog,' and they have all sorts of different ways they communicate through sound."

I cleared my throat. "The first thing I'm going to teach you is a coyote whine. You might or might not know that most coyotes live in packs, and they are super social, but they also have a definite pecking order. A whine is one of the ways that a coyote shows submission."

I cleared my throat again. Then I let out a whine mimicking the one I'd heard on the computer. It came out so authentic, it surprised even me. The audience clapped.

"The next sound I want to share is a greeting." Again, I let out a coyote sound that was something like *woo-ooooh-wow*. The judges were paying careful attention. One of them, an older woman wearing a fancy hat with a feather sticking out the top, nodded encouragingly, and my confidence grew. I went on to show them a warning growl, and then I decided to wrap up with a traditional howl.

"Scientists aren't exactly sure why coyotes howl, but they think it's an important source of identification for individual coyotes and probably also a signal of their location." I let out a long, hopeful howl that came from somewhere deep in my stomach.

The judges covered their ears, but they were smiling.

My confidence swelled, and I decided to add on a bonus. "Before I leave the stage, I want you all to work on your own coyote howls. There's no wrong way to do it. On the count of three, each of you needs to raise your chin and give me your best howl, okay?"

My palms were sweaty, and my pulse raced. This was either the best idea I ever had or the worst. "One," I said.

I wished I could take the whole thing back. "Two."

It would have been way better if I'd ended with my

own howl. At least I wouldn't have humiliated myself with a silent auditorium. "Three!"

The entire room filled with the sound of howling coyotes, and a wide smile spread across my face. The judges swiveled around and then, realizing everyone was participating, joined in the fun. The fancy-capped judge really threw herself into it—she raised her chin high in the air and howled with abandon.

When the noise died down, the auditorium rang out with loud applause. I took an impromptu bow and skipped off the stage.

Since I was already dressed for my interview, I stood in the wings and watched the next several contestants, including Leigh. Her routine was flawless, and she landed a series of flips at the end that made my jaw drop.

When she ran off the stage, it was all I could do not to wrap her in an excited hug. "Congratulations," I said.

"I thought your talent was singing," she said stiffly.

"Me too," I said, "but I changed my mind."

Hoping this conversation was the start of Leigh thawing, I opened my mouth to apologize, but she kept walking without giving me the chance.

A few minutes later, we lined up in the wings for a second time. Ava turned around and scanned my outfit head to toe. I braced myself for a nasty comment, but she only continued down the line as if tormenting me wasn't worth her time.

Somehow, that hurt worse than anything she might have said. My face flushed as heat spread through my body, radiating from a glowing ember that throbbed in my belly. No, the pain was lower than my belly. And deeper, more toward my back. It was like my insides had turned into a squirming pile of beetles, determined to scratch and claw their way out of my body. The sensation was a little like cramps, but it was the wrong time of the month. I squirmed uncomfortably, wondering what was happening.

Ava's name was called. I hoped she'd trip as she pranced onstage, but no such luck. She smiled and struck a perfect pose as the MC asked her a question about domestic violence. She spewed a bunch of statistics and talked about how important it was to make sure there were places victims could turn to for help. Her answer could have been straight from the speech our guidance counselor gave last year.

This was one of the topics Ms. Finley had encouraged us to prepare for, and I'd memorized all of the same statistics as Ava. I couldn't help but think the answer wasn't quite as simple as she made it sound. What if someone hadn't really hurt you yet but you were scared they were going to? What if they hurt someone around you? Or what if they didn't hurt you with their fists?

The cramping in my lower back crawled down toward my legs, making it hard to stand. I was trying to talk myself out of bolting when the MC called my name. I steeled myself. I could do this. I *had* to do this.

I marched onstage, taking care to avoid looking directly into the bright light.

"Good evening, Felicity," the announcer's voice boomed. "Could you please share with us your thoughts on world hunger?"

Ms. Finley had given us lots of statistics, like how ten percent of the world struggled with hunger and how something like twenty percent of kids weren't the right size because they didn't get enough to eat.

I leaned toward the microphone, but my stomach picked that moment to growl. Several people in the audience laughed. I scowled and adjusted my sling. Maybe it was funny to them, but there was nothing funny to me about an empty stomach. "That's a dumb question."

The audience gasped, but that wasn't my problem. They needed to hear the truth, not some facts I'd memorized to impress them. I continued. "Hunger sucks. It makes your stomach clench up tight and get all growly, and sometimes it makes your head hurt, and you have trouble thinking or focusing. I don't think anyone should have to go hungry. Ever."

I paused. The room was silent. That was good because I had more to say.

"Hunger isn't something that happens to kids over on the other side of the world. It's something that happens right here in the United States. It's a real problem. Did you know some kids don't even get enough food to grow properly?"

I thought I was finished after that, but Mom was always going on about big box stores and the system being set up to screw the small guys. "Oh, and people don't go hungry because they're lazy," I added. "They go hungry because they work really hard, but they aren't paid enough money to buy the gas they need to get to work, or to fix their cars when they break down, or to pay their rent when their kid gets sick and they're buried in hospital bills."

I peered down at the judges, trying to see if they were paying attention. They were. "So you know what I think about world hunger?" I asked. "I think it's a darn shame, and it's something we all need to work on fixing."

When I finished, I lifted my chin defiantly, waiting for them to boo me off the stage.

The auditorium filled with applause.

I squinted into the front row. The judges were smiling and nodding, and a few of them were making notes on the sheets in front of them. Ms. Finley sat in a chair off to the side, beaming. This time when our gazes met, she nodded in approval. *Take that, Ava Benson.*

CHAPTER SEVENTEEN

Back at my station, the worst of my pain had disappeared, leaving a fierce itch in its wake. I ripped off my dress and scratched frantically. When I reached around to my back, my fingers brushed against fur. What the . . . ?

My hand closed around something cordlike. My mind tried to wrap itself around what I was feeling. I tugged at the unidentified object. A sharp pain started at my tailbone and shot up my spine.

I whirled around and peered over my shoulder to get a view of my backside in the mirror. A tail stuck out of my underwear. A bushy, wiry tail. A tail attached to my body.

I covered my mouth and collapsed on my chair. The tail bulged under me like a dead animal, forcing me to adjust.

This wasn't possible. I was dreaming. Or someone was playing a trick on me. Maybe I was imagining it, the way I'd imagined having fangs. I jumped up and inspected myself in the mirror again.

The tail swished menacingly.

I tugged at it one more time, thinking it might come off if I pulled hard enough.

"Ouch!" This time, the pain forced me to holler out loud. Though I was only in undies, I sank to the floor, pulled my knees up to my chest, and wrapped my arms around them. The cool cast was hard against my warm skin. The tail twitched, then wrapped around me. My brain spun at warp speed. I didn't know if I should run away or ask a doctor or someone for help.

But I could imagine how that conversation would go. *Can you help me? I think I'm turning into a dog.*

What makes you think that? the doctor would ask.

I'd show them my tail.

Any other symptoms?

Lots of things had felt off lately. Strange growing pains, my bushy eyebrows and toes, my suddenly long nails, my super sniffer. The urge to bite people. There was also the fact that I seemed to be going color-blind.

Wait a minute. I gasped. I wasn't turning into a dog—I was turning into a coyote.

The truth of this hummed somewhere deep in my bones. All the changes to my body, my dreams, how easily and naturally I'd performed during the talent competition, how I could still see blue when everything else went gray—all of it had been driving toward this moment. But how? And why? I shook my head. Just because I admired coyotes didn't mean I wanted to *be* one.

This can't be happening. Ms. José-Fitzgerald had said animal-human hybrids were a scientific impossibility.

There had to be another explanation.

Magic, a voice in the back of my mind whispered. I brushed it aside. There was no such thing—I was sure of it. Then again, before today I was also sure that girls didn't turn into coyotes.

I sat huddled on the floor in disbelief until Ms. Kora announced that it was nearly time to line up for the evening gown portion of the competition. Moving robotically, I rose to my feet and pulled on my dress. The tail bulged, creating a huge lump.

I nearly collapsed back down on the floor, but I forced myself to stand up straight. I didn't know how or why this was happening to me, but I'd come this far. The audience—and the judges—seemed to like me. I wasn't going to give up on saving Mom or the baby now.

Think, I told myself. There had to be some way around this.

An idea started out fuzzy but then took shape in my mind. Ms. Finley had shone on the stage earlier. She didn't care one bit that she didn't look the same as the other queens. Then there was Imani, the beautiful lady at the shoe store. They both owned who they were. I was going to have to do the same, even if the judges did think it was all an act.

I peeled off the dress. After locating Mom's stitches, I

JESSICA VITALIS

bit the thread and tugged impatiently. The resulting hole
was small, but it'd have to do. I slipped the dress over my
head and used my good arm to pull my tail through.

It gave a little wag, as though happy to be free, which
was a seriously weird sensation. I wondered if I had any
control over it, but there was no time to think about that
now. I finished zipping my dress and pulled on my heels.
Then I slipped on my hoodie and tugged it down over my
tail before sprinting up and down the rows of stations,
trying to locate the girl I'd seen that morning with the
wolf ears.

She was just leaving to line up.

"Hi," I said, panting. She was wearing a sparkly sapphire-
blue evening gown. Her dark hair was pulled up in an
elaborate knot, and her eyes were highlighted with blue
eyeshadow, making them pop.

"You're the coyote-girl!"

I squirmed. "Yeah, about that. I need your help."

Her eyebrows shot up. "With what?"

I sucked in a deep breath. "I need to borrow your wolf
ears."

She frowned in confusion. "My wolf ears?"

"The ones you were wearing when you got here this
morning."

"My headband? What do you need that for?"

"I don't have time to explain now, but I'll get it back
to you when we're done. I promise."

"Sure," she said. "Have at it." She dug the headband out of her bag, which was embroidered with her name.

"Thanks, Angel," I said, tucking the headband in my front pocket as I hurried behind her. I slipped into line as the first contestant walked onto the stage.

"You can't go out like that," Ms. Kora said, waving her hand at my hoodie.

"I'm planning to take it off." I moved forward with the rest of the line.

"I need you to remove it now."

I gripped the headband inside the pocket. If Ms. Kora saw my tail, she'd never let me continue. "One more second."

As my name was called, I pulled off the hoodie, slipped on the headband, muttered a prayer to the hair gods that it didn't look too bad, and stepped into the bright lights.

The audience gasped. Instead of tucking my head, I lifted my chin. Ms. Finley's voice rang in my mind. If the judges wanted to know who I was, I'd show them. I pulled my cast close to my chest as I did my very best pageant walk. When I reached the front of the stage, I pivoted and did a little wiggle to show off my tail.

The audience tittered. Sensing I had them, I looked back and winked at the judges before sashaying off the stage.

"That was certainly . . . interesting," one of Ms. Kora's assistants said, covering the speaker on her headset.

I returned to my station, my insides twisting and bucking like a bronco. Nothing about this pageant had gone like I planned. The other girls had all been polished and pretty much perfect in every way. I hadn't been polished or perfect, but at least I'd been myself.

Hopefully, it was enough to convince the judges to crown their first-ever Coyote Queen.

An hour later, I was back onstage, lined up with the other twenty-nine contestants, waiting to find out if I was going home with the prize money. *Please,* I prayed. *I need to win this pageant.*

The MC cleared his throat. "Before we crown this year's Miss Tween Black Gold," he said, "it's traditional to award prizes for the best in each category. Winners will go home two hundred and fifty dollars richer."

I stood up taller. Two hundred and fifty dollars wouldn't save us from the boat, but it was more money than I'd ever had in my life.

"We'll start with the evening gown competition."

Even though I stood a better chance of riding an elephant in a rodeo than winning that category, I listened carefully.

Over on the side of the stage, the MC flipped open an envelope and pulled out a card.

"The winner of the evening gown competition is—"

He paused for dramatic effect. It worked. Every single

person in the crowd fell silent and waited for his answer.

"Ms. Hailey VanBeeker!"

The crowd applauded as the girl—Hailey—squealed.

I'd known I wouldn't win, but a sharp stab of disappointment tore through my stomach.

"Next up," the announcer said. "The interviews."

I peeked at the judges. They were watching the announcer.

"This award goes to—"

Again, he paused.

Get on with it, already!

"Angel Jones."

The audience clapped as the girl I'd borrowed the wolf ears from rushed forward to collect her prize.

I blinked back tears as the announcer moved on to the talent portion of the competition. It was dumb to get my hopes up, but some little part of me couldn't help it. They'd clapped super loud for me. That had to mean something, didn't it?

But how could I compete with all the other girls—girls who had *real* talent? Ava had a voice like liquid sunshine, and Leigh's tumbling had been perfect.

"The winner is . . ."

I squeezed my eyes shut.

"Ava Benson."

I opened my eyes. Ava rushed forward.

My body turned limp, like a wet spaghetti noodle.

The lights beat down on me. The room spun as my vision dimmed. If I couldn't win even one of the categories, what chance did I have of taking home the crown?

"Ladies and gentlemen," the announcer said for about the millionth time that night. "The moment you've been waiting for."

This time, I squeezed my eyes shut and prayed with every ounce of my soul. *Please, God, if you let me win, I'll never do anything wrong again. I'll be a perfect student, and I'll never complain about anything for as long as I live.*

"Third place goes to Amber Kingston."

The audience applauded politely. "Second place goes to . . ."

Please, I prayed. *I really need this. Please.*

"Alyssa Rice!"

I bowed my head and blinked. I wanted to win so badly I could practically feel the crown sitting on my head.

"The winner of this year's Miss Tween Black Gold pageant is—"

I sucked in a deep breath.

"Ava Benson!"

Ava squealed.

The audience clapped and cheered. Ms. Finley pinned a tiara on Ava's head and handed her a bouquet dripping with red roses. Balloons and streamers dropped from the

ceiling as the rest of the contestants rushed to congratulate her.

I hung back, watching the festivities like they were a
movie and not something happening right in front of me.
I doubted Ava even needed the money that came along
with the crown. And what about how mean she was?

Her satin sash was embroidered with the name of the
pageant. Miss Tween Black Gold, not Miss Coal. They'd
never tried to hide the fact that they didn't care about
anything except pretty packaging.

I'd been stupid, thinking I ever had a chance at winning. Even before the coyote stuff, I hadn't really stood a
chance. And now . . . there'd be no protecting Mom. Or
the baby. Heck, I wasn't sure I could even protect myself.
The crowd had enjoyed my tail when they thought it was
part of a costume. I had no idea what would happen if
anyone found out about my transformation, but I imagined it started with a whole lot of bullying and ended
with me locked in a laboratory full of scientists dissect-
ing my freakish body.

A bloated balloon floated toward me. I was about to
stomp on it when I noticed someone else standing alone
at the back of the stage.

Leigh. She choked back tears as she peered out at the
audience. My heart softened. I longed to tell her she didn't
have anything to worry about—she'd done a great job,
and her father would be proud of her no matter what.

But I was the last person she wanted to hear from right now. I kicked the red balloon. It shot up in the air, then floated back down to the stage as though it didn't have a care in the world. *Stupid thing.*

A movement caught my eye. Someone joined Leigh at the back of the stage. Not any old someone—Angel. Both girls smiled shyly, and then Angel said something that made Leigh's face light up.

My vision blurred. Leigh didn't need me—she never had. The only person who needed me was Mom, and I'd let her down. I rushed back to my station, desperate to get out of this gown, desperate to get out of this place. I longed for the quiet of my raft. I needed to think. To figure out what to do next. My tail twitched. Larry didn't care for me on the best of days. If he found out I was turning into a coyote, it was a safe bet he'd make good on his promise to find a spot on his property where a body would never be found.

A half hour later, Click poked her head into my station, indicating it was time to go. I'd already returned my borrowed wolf ears and wiped the makeup off my face with the wipes Click had provided.

I followed her to the lobby, grateful for the baggy sweats hiding my tail. The smile Angel had put on Leigh's face was gone, and dried tears streaked her cheeks. It was all I could do not to roll my eyes. Leigh was taking this whole pageant thing a bit far—she'd wanted to win to impress her dad, but it's not like winning was a matter of life and death. At least not for her.

She acted like I didn't exist as we lugged our bags and dresses across the parking lot. Snow had started to fall, but instead of soft, fluffy flakes, sharp ice pelted our faces, forcing us to squint through the dark.

A few spots down from Click's car, Ava and her mother placed her bags into a car so fancy it was practically a limousine.

Click and Leigh loaded our bags into the trunk. I hovered behind them, hoping Ava wouldn't notice me. The last thing I needed was to listen to her rub in her win.

"I'm starving," Ava was saying. "Can we stop for a cheeseburger on the way home to celebrate?"

Her mother's head snapped up. "Are you out of your mind? You barely fit in your gown as it was. And it's a good thing you won the talent award, because there's no way you could have won evening gowns. You were the heaviest girl onstage."

My mouth nearly dropped open. Ava didn't have a drop of fat on her.

"Please, Mom, I'm starved," she pleaded, wrapping her arms around herself to protect against the cold.

"There's some carrots in the ice chest," her mom said. "You can have a slice of turkey when we get home."

Ava must have felt me gaping. Her gaze swiveled

around to meet mine. "What are you looking at?"

"Congratulations," I said softly. "You were great tonight."

The last thing I saw before I slid inside Click's car and shut the door was the surprise on Ava's face.

CHAPTER EIGHTEEN

After we pulled into Click and Leigh's snow-covered driveway, I thanked Click for the ride and promised to pick up my outfits in the morning. Lights blazed inside our trailer, which wasn't really a surprise—Mom and Larry must have a million things to do to prepare for our departure.

I trudged through the storm, my dread growing with each step. Now that the pageant was over, now that I'd *lost*, I was going to have to face Larry—and his boat. I didn't even want to think about what would happen if he found out I'd competed. He'd probably tattoo TRAITOR right across my forehead.

When I opened the door, a blast of warm air greeted me. I blinked, trying to process the chaos spread across the room. Several boxes were tipped over, their contents spilled and smashed. The plant Mom had bought at the yard sale had obviously been thrown against the wall; the clay pot lay in shambles on the carpet, the brown, nearly dead leaves partially buried by a heap of thick, black soil.

Larry wasn't in the living room or kitchen, but his truck was parked outside, and Mom was asleep on the couch, so I figured he must be in their bedroom. I slipped off my shoes and began tiptoeing toward my room. Mom rustled and opened her eyes, which were puffy and red.

"Hi," she said, sitting up and smoothing her messy hair.

"Are you okay?" I scanned her for signs of new injuries.

She held a finger to her lips. "Fine," she said quietly. "How was the pageant?"

I longed to fall into her arms, to tell her about my day, to show her my toes and my tail and listen to her reassure me that we'd get to the bottom of it. But she was already dealing with enough—I didn't need to become one more problem she couldn't solve.

"The pageant was fine." I blinked back tears and motioned toward the mess. "What happened here?"

She rubbed her belly. "Larry had a long day. Needed to blow off some steam."

There she went, making excuses for him again. "You know it's only going to get worse if we get on that boat?"

"We've been over this," she said. "He's under a lot of pressure right now. Once he's out on the water, he'll settle down."

She raised a hand to push back her hair from her face. Her tank top revealed a mark under her arm that looked suspiciously like a bruise. "What's that?"

She dropped her arm. "Nothing," she said in a way that made it clear it was most definitely something. "I pinched myself."

"On what?" I was pressing my luck, but maybe if I made her say what happened out loud, it'd snap her out of whatever spell she was under.

"That's enough," Mom said, her voice warning me to let it go. "It's getting late and we have a long day tomorrow. Get some sleep."

A lone coyote howled in the far off, its ghostly voice hardly audible. The hair on my arms bristled.

Mom rubbed her bony arms as if fending off a chill. I hadn't noticed how much weight she'd lost recently. If it weren't for her stomach, she could almost be mistaken for a child.

She used to be so strong. She'd always made me feel safe. Cared for. When we lived out of The Miracle, she'd made sure I had the last few bites of ravioli or whatever meal we were splitting. When the heat had been shut off in one of our apartments, she'd given me her winter coat to sleep in. When a kid snapped my bra back in fourth grade, I'd called him a word I wasn't allowed to say and was sent to the principal's office. Instead of getting mad at me, Mom had insisted that the school make the boy apologize.

That all changed when Larry entered our lives. He'd snuffed out whatever fire had once burned inside her, and now she was stuck stumbling in the dark.

Maybe I could lead her to the light. "Mom, we can't get on that boat."

She sighed. "Go to bed, Fud."

I crossed my arms. "I'm serious. He's dangerous. He's already hurt you, and you know he'll do it again."

"Keep your voice down," Mom hissed, casting a fearful glance down the hall. "He's not dangerous. He just loses his temper sometimes."

I was done pretending with her. "He pushed me down the stairs."

I hadn't wanted to admit it before, had convinced myself that I wasn't sure. But now the truth burned deep in my belly. He *had* pushed me down the stairs, and I should have told the doctor. I hadn't spoken up then because I'd been too scared, but I had to tell the truth now.

"Fud, stop acting like a baby. I understand you're mad, but you can't go around accusing people of things just to get your way."

"It's the truth."

"I don't want to hear another word about it." She threw her arm over her face and lay back down. "Go to bed."

Heat built behind my eyes. I'd always thought that Mom and I were a pack—that like the mother coyote in my dream, she'd defend me to the death. Maybe that had been true back when it was only the two of us, but it obviously wasn't anymore. My insides felt like one of the mangled carcasses always lying on the side of the road.

Outside, another coyote howled, this one much closer. *I'll be back to the den soon,* it seemed to say.

I sprinted for the door and threw myself down the stairs. Sharp rocks poked the bottoms of my bare feet as I raced toward the bluff, ignoring the icy sleet biting at my face. My legs burned as I attacked the incline, but I refused to slow. As I ran, anger and rage and disappointment and sadness swirled inside me, igniting every atom in my body.

My skin didn't just itch—it burned like I'd been stung by a thousand fire ants. My senses sharpened. The crystalline taste of snow filled my mouth. The cold wind carried the scent of human pollution. Every drop exploded on my skin, small bombs of icy misery that sent shivers racing through me. I pressed on, ignoring the pain that pulsed as my feet slapped the frozen earth.

At the top, I slowed to a stop.

Warm tears cascaded down my cold face as my body continued to tingle.

I turned to Larry's trailer. The porchlight shone like a lighthouse warning passing ships of danger. I couldn't go back.

With a whimper, I tucked my tail between my legs and took off into the dark.

My feet burned, then numbed. I pulled my cast close to my chest and pumped my other arm as I sprinted at top speed, determined to put as much space between me and the trailer as possible. My lungs threatened to explode. Beads of sweat dripped down my forehead. My steps slowed. The angry wind howled as it nipped at my exposed skin.

I spun around, searching for a place to take refuge.

There wasn't so much as a gully to be found. I took off again, heading toward what I hoped was the highway, planning to follow it until I came across a house with a barn where I could hide. Or at least a ditch where I could shelter from the wind.

At last, the road came into view. I winced as I stepped onto the gravel shoulder. I longed to stop, to curl up in a tiny ball and sleep, but I forced myself to continue toward town. It took every bit of willpower to place one foot in front of the other. I was shivering now, my sweat cooled by the freezing air.

When I thought I couldn't take one more step, a drainage ditch opened alongside the road. I peered through the snow. Large boulders and sharp rocks littered the slope. Maybe the other side of the highway would be easier to manage.

I stumbled onto the asphalt. Something came into view—a pile in the middle of the road. Sleet slapped my face. The mound was furry. Light gray. Probably biscuit or sand-colored, but I had no way of knowing for sure. A distinctively darker patch of fur leered at me from the base of the tail. I gaped. It couldn't be the mother coyote from my dreams. And yet . . .

The coyote's skull was smashed, its body ripped open. I looked away, but not before I saw a tangled mess of blood and guts. Bile rose up in my throat. I scrambled down the bank on the other side of the road and into the ditch, gasping for air. Nearing the bottom, I tucked myself into the drainpipe's opening and wrapped my good arm around my knees, grateful to be out of the biting wind.

I should have been freezing. I *was* freezing, but something else was happening inside me, too. My body still tingled and itched, but now the single ember that had glowed in my stomach at the pageant turned into a full-on firepit, a burning pile of coals radiating a strange internal warmth. The skin on my arms prickled like individual strands of fur were attempting to break through. It was as if a coyote had been stuck inside me, and now it was determined to be set free.

I whimpered.

Coyotes might be smart and loyal and adept at surviving, but a transformation meant that I'd never get to meet my new sister or brother. Never see Leigh again. Never eat chocolate cake or go on a date or grow up to study science. Never hug Mom.

The image of the coyote on the highway haunted me.

My skin continued to prickle, and I bit back a long, frightened howl.

I closed my eyes, wondering if I'd be human or coyote when I opened them again.

My eyes snapped open. *Coyote. I am most definitely a coyote.* Panic fluttered in my chest, making it tighten. *Deep breaths. In. Out.* Something that sounded like a snore came from nearby. I sniffed the still-dark drainpipe for signs of danger. My eyes adjusted. There was no danger, only a pile of . . . pups? The very same pups I'd played with before. Wait a minute. That had been a dream. Was I dreaming now? I couldn't be—this felt too real.

I rose to four shaky legs and shook out my fur. My body felt strange. Off balance. But there was no denying the feel of my four paws pressed firmly against the ground. The sharp bite of the wind blowing in from the drainpipe's entrance. The milk-scented pups.

In, out. In, out.

One of the pups stirred, then opened its eyes. Spotting me, it let out an excited yelp and dove toward me, wiggling its bottom. The other pups rose, yawned, and then followed suit, yelping questions and comments.

"Where have you been?"

"Did you bring us any food?"

"I'm starving!"

"When's Mom coming back?"

"Will *she* bring us any food?"

The fur on my neck prickled as my doubts about whether this was real were replaced by worry. "How long has your mother been gone?"

"She left last night," the littlest pup yipped.

"She promised she'd be back before first light," the biggest pup said.

"Do you think something happened to her?" one of the middle pups asked.

I tried not to think about the mangled coyote on the highway as I licked the middle pup's face, my tongue smoothing its soft fur. "I'm sure she's fine," I lied.

"When's Dad going to be back?" the littlest one asked.

"Dad?" I sorted through images of the coyotes that had defended the den, wondering if one of them had been the pups' dad. Or maybe he was the one I'd heard howling recently. My brain glitched as I struggled, once again, to figure out whether this was real or a dream.

"He's been gone for two days. Said he caught wind of another coyote in the area and that he'd be back once he chased it off," the biggest pup said.

Another coyote in the area? I shivered. Did he mean me?

A growl sounded at the drainpipe's opening.

"Get away from my pups."

"Daddy!" The pups rushed toward a massive coyote

standing at the entrance. He dropped a limp animal—a skunk—at their feet and sniffed each of them as if reassuring himself they weren't harmed.

"You're not welcome here," he said, turning to me. "This is my territory. Get out. Now."

I dropped my head. "I mean them no harm. I knew—know—their mother." I stumbled over my words as my brain struggled to keep up.

He stepped toward me. A jagged scar ran down his ear. "I said *leave*."

I blinked. My vision wavered. The coyote standing in front of me morphed into a fish. His mouth opened and closed as he gaped at me silently. Waves rippled in the space between us.

I felt like I was swimming through a thick river of sludge, trying to separate truth from fantasy. These pups, they weren't real. But the coyote on the road, that had been.

The goldfish swam toward me. It changed again. It was still a fish but with Mom's face. The fish bumped into a glass wall, unable to reach me. I lunged forward but ran into the same pane of glass. Mom's face turned into Larry's. Then the body changed from a goldfish into a great white shark. Larry's mouth opened, revealing rows of razor-sharp teeth. The glass disappeared. He swam toward me. I tried to back up, but my feet refused to cooperate.

Just before his mouth snapped over my head, I opened my eyes.

I blinked them again. I was back in my body. My semi-human body. Everything that I'd been through crashed over me. I'd run away. My dream—the pups.

They weren't real, I reminded myself. But there'd been something else in my dream, something I couldn't quite remember. Something about fish. It felt important, like there was a message I was supposed to understand.

There'd been a shark. Larry. Goldfish. That was it!

The goldfish had looked exactly like Click's tattoo.

I hadn't understood what it meant while I was sleeping, but now everything that my brain had been processing came into focus. Mom was exactly like a goldfish—stuck swimming endless circles in a glass bowl. But being a coyote was no better. Out here in the desert, every day would be a fight for my survival. To find water, to find food. To avoid getting trapped or shot or run over.

The drainpipe closed in around me. I darted outside, my breath coming in heavy puffs. It was still the kind of dark that only happened when a thick layer of clouds hid the moon. The storm had nearly blown itself out, leaving behind only the faintest trace of snow.

I sniffed the chilly air, instinctively sorting through the scents that pummeled me, dismissing what didn't matter, searching out the information I needed to survive. A shiver of fear ran through me. The scent markers left by a nearby pack of coyotes were hostile—they carried a coded warning, telling me to turn around, to clear out while I still had the chance.

My tail drooped. The odds of finding a friendly pack weren't good. Without a pack to protect me, to teach me their ways, I'd be lucky to last more than a few days. I climbed out of the ditch, taking care not to let my glance stray to the coyote on the highway.

My skin itched. I had no idea what to do next. How long would my transformation take to complete? Where could I stay in the meantime? I climbed to the top of a nearby ridge, hoping the height would give me an idea where I was, what to do from here.

Off in the distance, a warm light glowed inside Click's trailer. I pictured myself curled up on her couch, my body warm, my stomach full of food. Then I saw Leigh stomping into her trailer without saying goodbye after the pageant.

The faint scent of a badger wafted through the night. Maybe it was the same one I'd seen with the coyote. They were two different species, but still, they knew enough to work together to survive, whether they were friends or not.

The light in Click's trailer flickered. This was no warning—it was an invitation. A promise. A warm, open hand in a cold, harsh world.

I started walking toward it, then broke into a run. A

rogue snowflake landed softly on my face, melting and mingling with my tears. When I reached the door, I beat against it with my fist, hoping Click was still awake.

She pulled aside the curtain and peered out, then yanked open the door.

"Fud," she said, pulling a bulky knitted sweater around her. "Is everything okay?"

Everything was definitely not okay, and it was probably going to get worse before it got better. I took a deep breath and pushed out the words that I'd been avoiding for so long. "I need help."

CHAPTER NINETEEN

Click wrapped me in a fuzzy robe as she prepared a pot of warm water to soak my frozen feet. It wasn't until I stopped shivering that she asked if I wanted to share what was going on.

I fumbled my way through everything that had happened since Larry's arrival in my life—the constant walking on eggshells, Mom's black eye, my broken arm—all of it.

Well, almost all of it. I left out the bit about turning into a coyote. I'd have to tell her—and Leigh—sooner or later, but there was only so much I could handle at the moment.

When I finished, she was quiet.

"Are you going to make me go back?" I whispered.

"It's far too late to sort anything out now," Click said briskly. "You can sleep on the couch, and we'll figure out what to do in the morning."

Her answer was obviously code for "Yes, you're going to have to go back," but I was too exhausted to do anything except follow her orders and snuggle into the couch's comfortable cushions.

When I opened my eyes, the room was bright and the air smelled of coffee. Click was standing at the stove flipping pancakes. Something was different. I could see the teal of Click's couch, the green of the plants hanging in the window, the bright orange of the tea-pot on the stove. My head felt clearer, lighter somehow, than it had in weeks. Smells weren't crowding my head, competing for attention. Everything was quieter, too. I hadn't realized how sharp my hearing had become. I sat up and adjusted the robe that had hidden my tail from Click the night before. I frowned, then squirmed on the couch, hardly able to believe what my mind was telling me. I peeked to make sure Click wasn't looking, then cautiously reached around to my backside. My tail was gone!

I wanted to rush to the bathroom to make sure, but someone banged at the door.

My terrified gaze met Click's. I imagined Larry barg-ing in, dragging me home by my hair, threatening Click if she got in the way. She nodded once as if to reassure me. My heart pounded like Larry's gloves hitting his punching bag.

Click turned off the stove and opened the door.

Mom stood in the doorway. I sat up taller, brimming

with hope. Maybe she'd come to tell me that she'd thought things over, that she'd decided against going with Larry.

She exchanged a few niceties with Click, and then her gaze landed on me. "Come on," she said, rubbing her lower back. "Let's go."

"Go where?" I'd go anywhere with her, as long as it wasn't also with Larry.

"We're all packed, and Larry isn't going to wait forever." Her eyes begged me not to put up a fuss.

A lump filled my throat. I'd always been a good daughter, done what I was told, tried to make her life easy. I should do that now, too.

"Why don't you come in and have a cup of tea?" Click said smoothly.

"I really don't have the time," Mom said. "Larry's ready to pull out."

"Larry can wait a few minutes," Click said, making it clear it wasn't an invitation so much as an order. She turned to me. "Fud, please go wake up Leigh. Your mom and I need a few minutes to chat."

I didn't want to leave the room, but a social worker had visited my class at school last year, and she'd said that our job was to ask for help when we needed it. I'd finally done my part—now I was going to have to trust Click to do hers.

Leigh was stirring when I entered her room. "Fud,"

she said, scowling as she sat up and clutched her blankets, "what are you doing here?"

I'd already gone through it all with her mom—I wasn't sure I could repeat everything again.

She must have seen something was really wrong because she jumped out of bed and guided me to sit. She sank down on the mattress beside me and rubbed my shoulders as if she didn't hate my guts.

I trembled. I hadn't cried last night talking to her mom, but now I fought back tears.

When she spoke again, her voice was gentle. "Are you okay?"

I'd been prepared for her anger. For a fight. For anything but kindness. She'd been a great friend to me, and I hadn't been honest with her. Heck, I hadn't even been honest with myself.

I let out a strangled sob.

"Fud, it's okay," Leigh said. "If this is about the boat, I understand why you didn't tell me. We can stay in touch, and you can visit—"

"It's not about the boat." At least not like she thought.

"Okay, well, whatever it is, we'll work it out."

A girl I'd only known for a couple of months—a girl who had every right to be mad at me—was offering to stand by me. Confronting Mom had taken every bit of courage I had, but she'd only made excuses for Larry, tried to trap me in the same bowl she was in. Didn't she know that goldfish spend their entire lives swimming in circles until one day they're found floating belly up?

I buried my face against Leigh's shoulder. She rubbed my back. "It's okay," she said, stroking my hair, offering silent support while I cried. I didn't deserve this kindness. Didn't deserve her friendship. The thought of leaving, of losing the only real friend I'd ever had, only made me cry harder.

When my sobs finally slowed, Leigh got me a wad of tissue from the bathroom. I blew my nose, filling the room with a loud honking sound. We both laughed, and I wiped away the rest of my tears.

She cocked her head toward the living room, listening. "Is someone here?"

I motioned for her to be quiet and tiptoed to the door, where I pressed my ear up against the wood.

Click's voice floated toward me. "I'm sure the police would be interested in hearing how Fud fell down the stairs."

I wrenched open the door and rushed to Mom's side. "I'm sorry," I said, falling to my knees. "I had to tell her. Please don't be mad."

Mom stroked my hair. "You've always been the brave one," she said, her voice breaking. "The strong one."

Mom thought I was brave and strong? I looked up, filled with hope. "Does that mean we're not getting on the boat?"

She exchanged a glance with Click. Leigh had come out and was standing at her mother's side.

"Your mom and I have been talking," Click said. "We think it might be for the best if you stay here with Leigh and me for the rest of the school year."

Leigh gasped.

My gaze jerked back to Mom's face to see if this was true.

She was staring into her mug like it was the most interesting thing she'd ever seen. Her thumb traced a circle around its rim.

I rose to my feet. "Mom?"

She rubbed her stomach. "It's only for the rest of the school year, so you can finish out seventh grade. We'll be back this summer to pick you up and introduce you to the baby."

"Don't do this," I begged. "Stay with me."

"You're both welcome as long as you need a place," Click said.

Suddenly, I was back onstage with the bright lights shining down on me as I waited for the judges to make their decision. To pick me.

Only I wasn't onstage, Mom wasn't a judge, and her decision was about a million times more important than some stupid pageant. She'd wanted me to stay quiet about Larry earlier, but that was when she thought we didn't have any other options. Hope fluttered around me, as bright and beautiful as a Viceroy butterfly.

"Please, Mom. Stay."

"Larry is this baby's father," she said, still avoiding my gaze. "But you'll be fine here. I'll leave your stuff in the trailer."

Click started talking about an attorney, using words like temporary guardianship and liability, but I didn't even try to follow the conversation. Mom's words had hit me like a bullet. I struggled to remain on my feet. Parents weren't supposed to abandon their children. It was true I'd be safer here than on the boat, but Mom had brought me into this world. Didn't that mean she was supposed to hold my hand as I walked through it?

A horn honked as Mom typed Larry's number into Click's phone. Mom stood up and offered me a watery smile as she set the phone down. "My chariot awaits."

She wrapped her arms around me. I stiffened, tempted to lash out, to unleash the full force of my anger. I wanted to use my words to drive a knife into her heart the same way she'd sliced open mine. But the little girl part of me, the part that still clung to the memory of the strong, protective mother I knew and loved, reminded me that I didn't know when I'd see her again.

Grief swelled inside my chest, pressing against my ribs as if they were prison bars. I melted into Mom's arms, trying to memorize the feel of her slender shoulders, her soft hair dusting my face.

She squeezed me tight.

I breathed in her familiar mint scent.

"I'm proud of you," she whispered.

She gave me one final squeeze, then pulled away.

Her footsteps rang through the silent trailer.

"Bon voyage," I murmured, fighting back hot tears.

With a last apologetic glance in my direction, she stepped outside.

The door clicked behind her, and she was gone.

CHAPTER TWENTY

Six weeks later, the school bell rang, signaling the end of the day. I tugged on the coat Click had lent me and headed for the bus. Performing in the pageant had reminded Leigh how much she loved gymnastics, and she'd joined the local team. Since she practiced every day after school, I rode the bus back to her trailer alone, which was fine because it gave me extra time to do homework.

I adjusted my backpack with the arm that had been broken. The cast was off, and my wrist was weaker than before but mostly back to normal. That wasn't the only thing that was back to normal—ever since that first night at Click's, there'd only been one time I'd thought maybe I was turning into a coyote again.

It'd happened when Tyler had thrown his arm around me at school a couple of weeks after the pageant. My vision had faded to gray, and there'd been a familiar tingle under my skin. But as soon as I told him that if he didn't leave me alone, I'd report him for harassment, he'd yanked his arm away. He'd kept his distance after that, and my coyote symptoms had disappeared.

"Fud! Hey, wait up," someone called as I exited the front of the school.

I spun around to see Lamonte making his way toward me. My insides tickled, but in a good way. I reached up to smooth my hair, which I'd started wearing down nearly every day. Not because it made other people think I was pretty, but because I liked it that way.

"Hi," Lamonte said.

"Hi," I said. "What's up?" We'd been talking a lot lately. He was just as nice as he'd been back when we'd played together in elementary school.

He cleared his throat and fiddled with the zipper on his coat. "The holiday lights display starts next week."

I'd never seen the holiday lights display, but it was apparently something where you purchased a ticket and then drove through a long series of lit displays out at some fancy golf course. I raised an eyebrow, trying to figure out why he was sharing this.

He stuffed his hands in his pockets. "My family always goes the first weekend. I was wondering if you wanted to join us?"

I couldn't help the grin that spread across my face. "I'd love to!"

His face lit up like he couldn't believe I'd agreed.

"Okay," he said. "Wow. Okay. I'll see you tomorrow." He jogged toward his bus.

I practically skipped the rest of the way to my bus. Today was my birthday, but I hadn't told anyone. Click and Leigh had already done so much for me, I didn't want them to feel like they had to do more. Still, it'd been weird going through the whole day without anybody saying anything. Lamonte's invitation felt a little like the universe whispering that it hadn't forgotten me.

At Click's trailer, I found a note that she was running errands, helped myself to a handful of barbeque chips, and sank down at the table to work on an English assignment. Click had cleared her desk out of the spare bedroom she'd used as an office, so I had a room of my own, complete with an extra-soft bed, a Star Wars comforter, and a shelf for my field guide, stuffed elephant, and shark teeth.

I loved sleeping in there, but I'd spent enough time hiding in my room—I liked working out here where I could take breaks to ask Click about her camera or chat with Leigh as she did her stretching. Even when they weren't home, their energy filled the space.

I was so focused on my work that I didn't realize how much time had passed, but I closed my notebook when Click's car pulled into the driveway. Seconds later, Leigh burst through the door, holding an enormous round cake covered in chocolate frosting.

"Happy Birthday!" she yelled. She set the cake down in front of me. It was one of those fancy grocery store cakes with at least three layers and covered in red, yellow, and blue balloons. *Happy Birthday Fud!* was written across the top in swirly red frosting.

"How did you know?"

"You had to give me your birthday when we filled out our pageant applications."

I blinked down at the cake. I'd been scared to ask for help, scared of losing Mom, scared of being alone. What I hadn't considered was that sometimes leaving one pack meant finding another. I never would have imagined that my new pack would be with Click and Leigh—even with the divorce, their lives had seemed pretty close to perfect.

But it turned out, Leigh's father hadn't shown up for the pageant. Apparently something had come up with work. I'd always thought money could solve all the world's problems, but I guess not even money could make a bad parent good.

"Can we have a slice now?" Leigh asked her mom, bouncing up and down.

"That's up to the birthday girl," Click said. "It's her special day."

Mom would never let me have cake before dinner. But Click was my guardian—at least for now. Family Services had gotten involved after Mom left, so I didn't know what the future would hold, but maybe part of growing up was learning which pieces of our past to hold on to and which to let go of. "Let's do it!"

"I suppose that means you want your present now, too?" Click asked in a teasing voice.

I was too overwhelmed to speak.

She smiled as she pulled a large gift bag from behind the paper grocery bag she'd set on the counter. "Happy birthday, Fud."

I pushed aside the tissue paper and gasped. A brand-new black backpack!

"Unzip it," Leigh said, hopping up and down.

I pulled out an enormous jar of strawberry jam with a big red bow on top. I'd polished off their strawberry jam the week before and hadn't had the courage to ask if they'd buy more.

"That's from me," Leigh said.

I squeezed them both to my chest. "These are the best gifts ever!"

Click laughed. "I doubt that, but I'm glad you're happy."

Her phone buzzed with a text. She peeked at the screen. "It's for you," she said, passing the phone over.

"Happy Birthday!" Mom's message read. "I miss you." She'd attached a picture of herself standing in front of what I was pretty sure was the St. Louis Arch. Her belly had grown, but her face was thinner than before. A fresh wave of hurt rolled over me. She was supposed to be here celebrating by my side, not standing under an arch a thousand miles away.

My hands trembled as I typed out a response. "Thank you. I miss you, too."

I clicked Send before I could change my mind. My message was only partly true—the mom I missed had actually left long before this mom had sailed off with Larry. But I couldn't change her decision any more than I could make her turn back into the mother I wanted her to be.

I reminded myself that she'd left me here to protect me. That wasn't the kind of mothering I wanted, but at least it was something.

I handed the phone back to Click, who had been busy lighting the thirteen candles on top of my cake. The candles flickered, each one a tiny beacon, a promise of a bright future to come. Click's smooth, gentle voice harmonized with Leigh's slightly off-key one as they sang "Happy Birthday" at the top of their lungs.

Leigh jumped up and down after they finished. "Make a wish!"

At first, I didn't know what to wish for. Then something stirred deep in my chest. I'd never believed in magic, but there was no other explanation for what I'd experienced. The coyote stuff would always be a part of me, but I was pretty sure it wouldn't try to take over again anytime soon. It seemed content to prowl the open spaces between my cells, a secret reminder of the strength I always had inside me. I closed my eyes. *I wish that one day, Mom finds a bit of coyote magic hiding inside of her, too.*

I blew out every one of my candles in one long breath. Click and Leigh clapped and cheered, then Click cut through the thick brown frosting, carving the spongy chocolate cake into slices. She slid a wedge onto a plate and set it in front of me. My eyes widened when I saw that she'd given me the largest piece—and the one with the most frosting on top. I stuffed a giant bite in my mouth, moaning with pleasure as the sweet chocolate exploded on my tongue.

A mischievous twinkle lit Leigh's eyes. She used her finger to dab frosting on my nose.

"Hey!" I swiped at my cake and then smeared a streak on her cheek.

We both scooped up more frosting and turned toward Click.

"Oh no, you two keep me out of this," she said, holding up her hands and stepping back from the table.

We all laughed as a different kind of magic swirled around us—one that had nothing to do with coyotes.

AUTHOR'S NOTE

You may be wondering how much of this story, which has been more than twenty years in the making, is true. The answer is more complicated than it might first appear. Obviously, I have never turned into a coyote. I've also never participated in a beauty pageant (although I was a judge for one). Miss Tween Black Gold doesn't exist (if it did, it would almost certainly narrow the field of girls into a set of finalists before declaring a winner; I chose to take liberties with this, and other pageant logistics, to suit my story). Likewise, there is no Great Plains Golden Ring competition, and boxing champions typically receive belts rather than rings. The story is fictional in another important sense as well: all of the characters and their histories are entirely made up.

That being said, many of Fud's heartaches mirror the pain from my own childhood, which was spent on the fringes of society. I'd lived in nearly two dozen different places before fourth grade, including various apartments, trailers (including one in rural Wyoming, where this story is set), a school bus, a camper, and a one-room cabin with no electricity or running water. I was often hungry and didn't feel safe physically or emotionally. Some of Fud's experiences, like sleeping in a yellow raft, being forced to scrub the bathroom with her toothbrush, and the scene at the first hospital, are based on my own experiences. The coyotes in this story are inspired by the howling coyotes that prowled around our one-room cabin (near the Wyoming border).

Fud's name is also based on personal experience; as a child, an adult in my life insisted on calling me Fud—he found my passionate hatred of the nickname entertaining. When he brought home a sweet little German shepherd, I immediately got to work naming it, only to have him declare that the puppy's name would be Fud, which he undoubtedly thought hilarious but seemed to me an unspeakable cruelty. I suppose naming my main character Fud in this story is an attempt to reclaim my power.

The boat in this story is real; the enormous, rusted-out clunker appeared in our yard when we settled down for a short time around middle school. Though plans to fix it up and sail it down the Mississippi never came to fruition, the threat hung over me like a heavy cloud.

I turned to books for solace, losing myself in worlds real and imagined for hours each day. These stories taught me that there was an entire world I knew nothing about, but they all lacked one thing: kids like me.

Kids who were poor, kids who were hungry, kids who felt scared, helpless, trapped, or unseen—kids in need of hope.

If you are one of those kids, know this: there is hope—and help—available. If you are experiencing (or have experienced) physical or emotional abuse, talk to a trusted adult—if they don't believe you or won't help, talk to a teacher, principal, counselor, nurse, or doctor. They are all mandated reporters, which means they are required by law to report abuse. You can also call the National Child Abuse Hotline at 1-800-422-4453. *No one has the right to hurt you, and if they do, you have the right to seek help.*

If you are a kid and have witnessed (or suspect) that a minor you know is being abused, report it to a trusted adult immediately. *It's not your responsibility to decide if the situation is "bad enough" to deserve attention.*

Adults who witness or suspect abuse should call their local child protective services agency or the National Child Abuse Hotline listed above. If the child is in immediate danger, call 911. (Please note: in some states, all citizens are required by law to report suspected abuse, regardless of whether you work in an industry with a "mandated reporter" designation.)

It should also be noted that although poverty and abuse are intertwined in my story, they do not automatically go hand in hand; there are a great number of loving and attentive parents who struggle to make ends meet, just as there are a great number of financially stable parents who inflict serious harm upon their children. It is also important to note that some of Larry's abusive behavior stems from his alcoholism. Of course not all alcoholics are violent and/or emotionally abusive, and not all abusers are alcoholics. But if you live with or suffer the consequences of another person's drinking, remember that it's a disease. *You didn't cause it, and you can't control it.* And whether or not the alcoholic is abusive, the disease still affects you—living with an alcoholic makes you feel small and invisible and impacts your life in ways you may not even be aware of. Alateen is a support group for kids 13–18 (although some groups allow younger children to attend) that can help you understand and recover from the effects of living with this disease. To learn more or find a group near you, go to: https://al-anon.org/newcomers/teen-corner-alateen.

For those of you who have never experienced abuse, I realize Fud's story may have been difficult to read, but according to the CDC, in the United States at least "one in seven children experienced child abuse or neglect in the last year," and according to Childhelp, "nearly five children die in the United States *each day* as a result of child abuse." For the hundreds of thousands of children experiencing abuse in our country each year, Fud's story isn't a work of fiction—it's their reality.

Fortunately, there are a number of organizations working to eliminate child abuse and end domestic violence, and you can help. If you have the resources, encourage your family to support local or national groups dedicated to eliminating domestic abuse and protecting children, either through financial donations or by volunteering your time. Childhelp, CASA/GAL Association for Children (CASA/GAL stands for Court Appointed Special Advocate and guardian ad litem), and the NCADV (National Coalition Against Domestic Violence) are good places to start.

Finally, please keep in mind that we never know what people are dealing with in their private lives. Kids who are struggling academically or socially aren't bad kids. But they may be kids who are trapped in bad situations. A smile or a small act of kindness could make all the difference.

ACKNOWLEDGMENTS

When I lived in Georgia, a quote on my therapist's wall read, "Our stories shape us." My story certainly shaped me and it helped shape this book. While it is not a "true" story, many of Fud's heartaches mirror the pain from my own childhood. To my family, friends, and everyone who ever lifted me up, gave me a soft spot to land, or helped me heal, thank you.

An especially enormous thank-you goes out to the entire pack at Greenwillow / HarperCollins. Martha Mihalick, you are truly an editor extraordinaire. Paul Zakris, Lois Adams, Arianna Robinson, Taylan Salvati, and Robby Imfeld, thank you for your tireless efforts during what I know has been a challenging couple of years. Sarah Thomson and Barbara Rounds-Smith, thank you for your careful copy edits and proofreading. Dion MBD, this cover is nothing short of extraordinary; you perfectly captured Fud in all of her isolation and determination. To my expert reader, thank you for the feedback on how Fud's situation might have unfolded in the real world and the information in my author's note; any errors are my own. Sara Crowe, thank you for working your own kind of magic to help bring this story to the world.

Juliana Brandt, Gabrielle Byrne, Kami Kinard, Sue Berk Koch, Rebecca Petruck, Donna Rasmussen, Amanda Rawson-Hill, Eileen Schnabel, Saba Sulaiman, Jaiden Vitalis, and Stefanie Wass, thank you for the thoughtful insights that helped shape this book. A special shout-out to Julie Artz, who has cheered for this story since it first landed in her inbox (and has read it more times than I can count!). To the members of the Drakainas and Women Who Write: thank you not only for your professional support and unwavering belief in this book, but also for your friendship.

Thank you also to the countless other friends and family who critiqued previous versions of this story and/ or my even earlier attempts at writing a memoir—there are too many of you to name individually without panicking that I missed someone, but without the feedback from each and every one of you, I might never have found the story I was really trying to tell. Middle Grade Authorcade members—it's already been a great ride, and I look forward to many more years driving home our love of books to young readers.

Thank you to my mother, who has always supported my writing journey unconditionally, and to all my siblings—I love you. I also want to extend an enormous thank you to Adam, Jaiden, and Sienna—you are the light shining in my dark.

Finally, to my readers: thank you for opening your hearts and letting my stories in. While this book is about coyote magic on the surface, it's really about two other kinds of magic—the kind that comes from loving and believing in yourself, and the kind that comes from being surrounded by people who love you. May you all find plenty of both kinds of magic in your life.